The Most Guilty

M. A. SIMONETTI

Those who are caught are not always the most guilty.
—Aesop

ISBN: 1543270050
ISBN 13: 9781543270051
Library of Congress Control Number: 2017902877

Createspace Independent Publishing Platform
North Charleston, South Carolina

Also by M. A. Simonetti

The Third Side
The Fox's Watch

For Anthony

Non mangia qualcosa piu grossa della tua testa!

Chapter One

My 9:00 a.m. appointment was quite certain that she didn't need my help.

"I've no idea why my daughter sent you here, Alana. I'm sixty years old and capable of having coffee with a nice man without a chaperone." Marjorie Dunham squinted in the sunlight as she spoke. The morning was a perfect blend of sunshine and a cool breeze. We sat outside the Starbucks at Broad Beach Road, each of us cradling a cup. Marjorie had a stylish new haircut and wore bright lipstick. She was a little too dressed up, but then her last date had been sometime around 1976.

Still, she didn't look bad for her age, which I knew was not sixty. "Your daughter's worried that you're naive. And you're sixty-four."

My name was Alana Fox, and I'd lived in Malibu for over twenty-five years. People who understood the value of a stellar social circle hired me to help them broaden their horizons. If you thought this was frivolous, then you hadn't tried to make new friends after a certain age. Or you were too young to understand how the world really worked.

Marjorie Dunham was recently divorced after thirty-nine years of marriage. She was typical of most of the women I work with—suddenly single, over sixty, and terrified.

I was divorced myself, so I understood how she felt. After putting in thirty-nine years, Marjorie figured her work was done. It was time to relax, travel with the hubby, and maybe let her figure go. But the hubby had different plans, and all of them involved another woman. So Marjorie had to lawyer up and fight for enough assets to last the rest of her life. She was now sick and tired of paying

1

people to tell her how to live and how to act. She was determined to prove she could take care of herself, thank you very much.

Unfortunately, the world had changed since Marjorie last ventured out on a date as a single woman. When the daughter learned her mother had signed up for an online dating service, I received a frantic call to intervene.

"Alana, I'm sure your services are very useful to some people," Marjorie insisted. "But I can fend for myself. My daughter is being overprotective."

"How do you know this guy you're meeting is telling the truth?"

"He looks like a lovely man. Here's his picture." Marjorie held up her cell phone. On the screen was a full-length photo of a man with a gray beard and silver hair. He was in decent enough shape, and he held a small dog in his arms. "See? He owns a dog. It's name is Danny Boy. And look at his shoes! My mother always said you can tell a lot about a man by the shoes he wears."

"How do you know this is him?"

"Why would he post a picture of someone else?"

I took her phone away and pulled up her profile. "Why did you list your age as fifty-eight?"

Marjorie grabbed the phone back in a hurry. "That's none of your business. And by the way, this website only cost me ninety-nine dollars. I don't need to pay seventy-five hundred dollars to meet new people. I'm a very good judge of character."

"Fine, then. Do this your way, but I promised your daughter that I'd keep an eye on you. I'll sit over there and pretend I don't know you."

I moved to an empty table and waited for the lovely man to show up.

I didn't have to wait long. The guy from Marjorie's photo arrived, wearing good shoes and leading his dog on a leash. The dog was some kind of mixed breed, bigger than a Chihuahua but smaller than a beagle. The guy spotted Marjorie right off the bat.

"You must be Marjorie! I'm Barry Stabler. So nice to meet you in person."

Barry took Marjorie's hand and gave it a kiss. He took the seat right next to her, which provided me a decent view of both of them. I busied myself by searching my phone for the plot summary of *Looking for Mr. Goodbar*.

"It is lovely to meet you too, Barry. Is this Danny Boy?"

"This is Danny Boy. Danny, meet Marjorie."

Danny Boy raised his paw for Marjorie to shake.

"I got him at the SPCA when my daughter moved out," Barry went on. "I hated living alone, and this little guy hated living in the shelter. I don't know who rescued whom. He has my back, like all my buddies in the corps did fifty years ago."

Barry was pretty smooth—I'll give him that. Thirty seconds into the conversation, and he'd let Marjorie know that he was in his late sixties, a father, a veteran, and an animal lover. His hair and beard were professionally trimmed, and his nails were clean and neat. And Marjorie's mother would have approved of his shoes—Tod's driving moccasins.

Marjorie ate it up.

"How long have you lived in Malibu, Barry?"

"Moved here just about a year ago from the Valley. Once my daughter moved out, I didn't need the big house anymore. I decided to get closer to nature and move to the beach."

"You've found it easy to make friends?"

Marjorie asked this of Barry, but I knew the question was aimed at me.

"Moved here just about a year ago from the Valley. Once my daughter moved out, I didn't need the big house anymore. Danny and I talk to everyone. Especially the ladies."

The repeated answer was odd, but given Barry's age, it was possible that he didn't hear Marjorie's question correctly. Marjorie must have thought so, too. She leaned in closer and asked again.

"Have you found it easy to make friends here in Malibu?"

I gave her an A for effort.

"Yes, I have. Danny and I just love the ladies. You know, you ladies are so lucky to live here in the States. You know what life is like for women in Southeast Asia?"

Barry didn't wait for Marjorie to answer. He went right ahead and fulfilled Marjorie's daughter's fears. And then some.

"All those commies keep them suppressed. They keep the vote away from the women and lock them indoors. That's what's wrong with this world. Danny and I knew as soon as we saw your profile that you were a lady who wouldn't stand for that crap. Didn't we, Danny Boy?"

Marjorie's faith in a man's good shoes disappeared with that. I could tell by the way she grabbed her handbag and clutched it to her chest. I suspected she was close to changing her mind about accepting my help, but I stayed seated and waited for the actual request. I was very polite that way.

I didn't stay seated for long.

Barry pulled Danny Boy up onto his lap and kissed the dog full on the lips. Then he pushed the dog up to Marjorie's face.

"Give Danny Boy a kiss. He loves American ladies as much as I do."

Marjorie jerked back and put her bag between her face and the dog. Danny Boy's snout bashed up against the bag, leaving a snotty smudge on the leather. Marjorie gasped.

I felt her pain. The bag was a Birkin.

Marjorie glanced at me and mouthed, "Help!"

I was there in an instant.

"Marjorie! How good to see you!"

I pulled her to her feet, gave her a hug, and whispered in her ear, "Just go along with me."

"And who is this handsome devil?" I asked.

"This, this is Barry. Barry, this is…"

"Nice to meet you, Barry!"

I pushed Marjorie away and stuck out my hand.

"I'm Teri Ford, president of the Malibu Communist Party," I lied. "Are you new in town, Barry? You do know there is a gubernatorial election coming up? We're looking for all the help we can get."

Barry ignored my outstretched hand. He grabbed Danny Boy up in one swift move and made it to the parking lot faster than you can say "God Bless America."

I sat down in Barry's empty seat.

Marjorie let out a sigh and slumped back in her chair. After a moment, she opened her snotty handbag.

"Seventy-five hundred, you say? Will you take a check?"

Chapter Two

I walked Marjorie to her car and told her that I would be in touch soon. I promised to tell her daughter that Marjorie had opted to not meet with the Guy with Nice Shoes and decided to work with me instead. I reassured Marjorie that she would meet a truly nice man in the future, but she had to trust my methods to make that happen. I was good enough at what I did that Marjorie drove away with a smile on her face, despite being seventy-five hundred dollars poorer.

My plan for Marjorie was to first make certain that her check cleared. Then I would return to my office and start to work on reintroducing her to society as a single gal. To do that, I had to reintroduce Marjorie to herself. After thirty-nine years as Mrs. Dunham, she would need a little time to get comfortable as Ms. Dunham—a task best accomplished through girlfriends. I knew a group of Malibu divorcées and widows whose idea of a good time was to hire a driver to haul them to the outlet mall in Camarillo and then hop from one Happy Hour to the next on the way back home.

Marjorie was just a couple of boozy shopping trips away from a new circle of friends.

But that seventy-five hundred she'd just spent would get her more than new shoes and cocktails. I would show her how to cultivate new interests, how to travel alone, how to entertain without a man around to start the barbecue. It would take the better part of a year, but Marjorie would emerge with a new outlook on life. Then, and only then, would I approach the subject of bringing a new guy into her life.

I knew how to help people start anew because I had had to reorder my social life once, too. My marriage ended after twenty years when my husband left me for Little Miss Tight Buns. In the divorce, I lost the house and the business we'd built. I had to figure out how to live on my own in a town that now sported two Mrs. Foxes. Rebuilding my life was only doable because I held onto the friends.

I convinced the friends to shut out Little Miss Tight Buns from any Malibu social gathering, including the high school car wash. (Yes, I am a poor loser—just ask my ex-husband.) But in the process of shutting out LMTB, I learned to use my connections to help Malibu newcomers build new social circles. Before long, I had a thriving new business. And LMTB was forced to drive down Pacific Coast Highway (PCH) into Santa Monica for her coffee dates—which she still does, ten years later.

As I unlocked the door to my car, my phone rang. The ring tone was the only one I always answered.

"Hi, Jorjana!" I answered the phone expecting Jorjana York to be on the other end.

"Pardon me, Mrs. Fox. This is Perry speaking."

Perry is Jorjana's social secretary.

My stomach turned.

"Is Jorjana OK?"

"Oh yes, no need to worry. Mrs. York is quite well."

"Thank God." The adrenaline rush that had turned my stomach now drained away and made my legs weak. I leaned against my car for support.

Jorjana York was confined to a wheelchair, and her health was fragile. My alarm rose, because while it wasn't unheard of for Perry to call me, it was rare. And it usually happened when Jorjana fell ill.

"Mrs. York requests that you join her in the Dining Hall for the meeting about tonight's dinner. There has been an unexpected development."

I looked at my watch. Just 10:00 a.m. I knew Jorjana had a meeting to finalize the plans for a dinner she was hosting that evening. It wasn't like this was Jorjana's first dinner party. Surely she could handle it by herself.

"Isn't she just confirming the details? Why does she need my help with that?"

"Yes, well, Mr. Wheeler himself is here for the meeting."

Ah, that explained everything.

"Mr. Wheeler" was Ken Wheeler. Ken was tall, rich, and handsome, which apparently qualified him to run for governor of California. Jorjana and I had met him at a party earlier in the year. Jorjana loved the guy. Me, not so much. But Jorjana was so convinced that Ken could save California from itself that she was hell-bent on introducing him to anyone who would listen. Thus the intimate dinner for 250 that night at the York Estate.

I'd spent the last couple of months listening to Jorjana's tales of woe in organizing this shindig. Jorjana never said anything bad about anyone, but she came close to it when venting about the frustrations of dealing with Ken and his campaign team. I lost track of how many times the date of the event changed. Ken was to give a policy speech, and then he wasn't. Ken was attending alone, and then his family was tagging along. The guy had the attention span of a gnat, so I started referring to him as the Nitwit. And every last one of his staff members was barely old enough to vote. I dubbed them the Brats. I never said this to Jorjana, of course. In spite of the chaos, she was convinced he was the leader that California needed.

I couldn't imagine what nonsense the Brats had dreamt up, but Ken's presence at the meeting ensured mayhem would reign. No wonder Jorjana needed help.

"I'll be there in ten minutes," I told Perry.

I hopped in my car and headed south on PCH. The day was shaping up to be spectacular, as the sun shone merrily over the deep-blue ocean. I'd lived in Malibu all of my adult life, and I never tired of the vastness of the Pacific Ocean or the harsh beauty of the Santa Monica Mountains. As breathtaking as Malibu was, it was a tough place to live. The first Malibu residents were the Chumash Indians, who spent their time fishing and dancing on the beach. They'd had the good sense not to build on the land.

Good sense went out the door as settlers ran out of space in the Los Angeles Basin. Today, homes lined up shoulder to shoulder along Malibu's western shore. If you had the money to live here, you'd better buy two homes, because your first one would most likely be swept out to sea or burned to a crisp in a wildfire or buried in a mudslide. Mother Nature took no prisoners in Malibu.

Natural disasters aside, there was nowhere else I would rather be than Malibu on a clear, sunny day. Especially when there was no traffic. I made it to Jorjana's place in record time.

The York Estate sits on a parcel of land slightly smaller than Central Park. The house—all twenty-five thousand square feet of it—perches at the edge of a bluff and offers a better than average view of the Pacific Ocean and downtown Malibu. The bluff is known as Bella's Bluff—named after the daughter Jorjana and Franklin York lost in a freak accident. That same accident put Jorjana in a wheelchair. Franklin escaped without physical injury, but the damage to his psyche was irreparable.

I met Jorjana when my husband and I first moved to Malibu. The Yorks lived next door while they built the York Estate. Jorjana and I became fast friends. Thirty years later, she was the one whose name I entered on those forms requiring next of kin.

As close as we were, you would think I would have unfettered access to her house. Alas, even I had to go through a security checkpoint to get inside.

A gate guards the entrance to the Estate and is situated at the foot of the bluff. It is an eighteen-foot wrought iron affair, with all the scrolls and gilding one would expect. A fence surrounds the property, stands ten feet high, and sports metal tips not unlike arrowheads. Gilded, of course.

A metal box perched on a wrought iron post outside the gate. I pulled up to it and pushed a large green button. I smiled and waved at a security camera mounted to the fence. The camera moved up and down and then back and forth. Someone in the security office in the Main House confirms the identity of all visitors. They all know me.

The gate swung open anyway.

The drive from the gate to the Main House winds back and forth up the bluff. It takes several minutes to negotiate the climb. The view gets increasingly better the higher up you travel. Eventually, the drive leads away from the view and delivers you to the Main House.

The front entrance faces away from the bluff and sports a regal porte cochere designed to protect visitors from the unlikely event of rainfall. As I approached, I spotted a fleet of black Cadillac Escalades and one white Lincoln Navigator. I figured the SUVs delivered Ken Wheeler and the Brats to the meeting.

Alongside the Caddies stood two men the size of Paul Bunyan, dressed in black T-shirts and black cargo pants. They sported military-grade haircuts and carried holstered guns. The Bunyans were a new development. And unnecessary in my opinion. The York Estate boasted a top-notch security staff. Where the hell did Ken Wheeler think he was? Beverly Hills?

The Bunyans all but ignored me as I parked behind the Navigator. I had, after all, been cleared for access at the front gate. I gathered my bag and exited the car.

And stopped dead in my tracks.

I couldn't believe my eyes. The Navigator bore personalized license plates.

The plates read MRSFOX.

Yup, the Lincoln Navigator parked outside Jorjana's home belonged to none other than Little Miss Tight Buns.

Suffice it to say, this displeased me.

Some women came to terms with their ex-husbands' new wives. Some women could rise above the humiliation, the hurt and the betrayal. Some women even got to the point where they could be in the same room with the new wife and speak civilly to her.

I am not one of those women. From the day my husband said he was leaving, until now, I treated my husband's new young wife like crap on the bottom of my shoe. Which is why I did everything in my power to cut her off from the social scene in Malibu. It hadn't been easy, mind you. I twisted arms and made threats. There may have been a restraining order along the way. In the end, I made certain that she and I did not run in the same circles. So she had never crossed the threshold at the York Estate.

Until now.

I knew Jorjana would never, ever invite Little Miss Tight Buns into her home. This madness stunk of Ken Wheeler. What was the Nitwit thinking?

I threw my keys at the valet and headed straight for the Dining Hall.

The York Dining Hall seats one hundred. Ninety-eight chairs line the table, which is made from one long slab of redwood. One wall is all glass and looks out over the pool.

The other wall sports Franklin York's hunting trophies— the collateral damage of Franklin's damaged psyche. Mounted heads of antelope, deer, musk oxen, hyenas, a rhino, and one sad moose are mounted on display. The sight of all those glass eyes so unnerved Jorjana that she had had each head fitted with custom-made sunglasses.

At the far end of the table sat a dozen or so Brats, each one staring at a laptop and typing at warp speed. The head Brat was a young guy I knew as Luke. Luke was busying himself snapping photos of Ken Wheeler with a cell phone.

Ken stood at the head of the table with papers in hand. He was practicing a speech—a lot of nonsense about adding jobs, increasing funding for schools, and promising everyone a puppy. As best as I could tell, Ken's plans only differed from the other party's in that they promised kittens.

Jorjana sat in her wheelchair listening to every word Ken said. Her hands were folded in her lap. Her feet were tucked into padded boots. She wore an embroidered red tunic and white pants. Her curly black hair bounced on her shoulders as she nodded her head in approval.

I had to admit the Nitwit was savvy enough to know whom to cultivate. Jorjana York's connections spread well beyond the shores of Malibu. She grew up with a father in the diplomatic corps, so she can get a head of state on the phone faster than you can say "Wheeler for President Next Time," which explained why Ken was courting Jorjana's favor. As a Northern Californian, Ken did not have the connections he needed to gather a following in Southern California. Jorjana had the clout to put him in front of the most influential voters in Malibu.

A basic Google search about Ken Wheeler would tell you that he was born handsome and grew tall. A basketball scholarship got him to Stanford, where he met the daughter of the second-richest man in San Francisco. He married the daughter and then set about to make his own money. He fathered three sons, sold his company for gazillions, and set up a charitable foundation. All of this was done in Northern California, where he was as well known as the Golden Gate Bridge.

Tonight Jorjana would give him the chance to make a personal connection with well-connected people in Malibu. It was a unique opportunity. I hoped like hell that Ken Wheeler appreciated it. Because he sure wasn't savvy enough to know not to bring MRSFOX to the York Estate.

Little Miss Tight Buns sat across the table from Jorjana. She was blond, of course, and midthirties. She wore her hair a good six inches longer than was becoming for a woman of her age, but no one had ever accused her of good taste. There was a pad of paper and a pen on the table in front of her, as if she was capable of taking notes and breathing at the same time. She, too, nodded as Ken laid out his plans for the state.

It was a good thing it took a while to walk from the entry of the Dining Hall to the far end of the table. I needed the time to gather my wits.

Jorjana's gaze shifted from Ken, and that's when she spotted me. She sent a half-smile my way. And then a small nod. She was telling me she was happy to see me and that I was to follow her lead. After years of entertaining together, Jorjana and I have developed a secret code that allows us to communicate without involving—or embarrassing—others.

Apparently Jorjana had a plan. It was a good thing that she did, because my wits had not gathered by the time I made it to her side.

"...and that, my friends, is why I am asking for your support this evening."

Ken finished the speech with a bow of his head.

Jorjana looked back at him. "That was very good, Ken!" She clapped her approval.

Ken managed to produce a blush to accessorize his bow.

"I'm glad you approve, Jorjana," Ken said. "I had to really work at making it short and sweet."

"You managed to address the important topics without weighing down your message in details. Our guests will have all the information they will need," Jorjana said. And then she turned her attention to me. "Now that Alana has joined us, shall we begin the meeting?"

"Yes, of course. Good morning, Alana. It's good to see you," Ken said as he took a seat. The head Brat snapped away like Ken had just set a world record in sitting down.

Little Miss Tight Buns said nothing as she picked up her pen and shot a smug smile my way. Like she knew something I didn't. I did not give her the satisfaction of knowing she irritated me. I got points for that.

"Ken, would you please share with us the new idea you have for this evening's dinner?" Jorjana asked.

"Sure thing." Ken leaned forward in his seat, his face as eager as a Labrador chasing a ball. "Alana, do you know Tori?"

Tori is Little Miss Tight Buns's given name.

He asked this of me. He actually asked me, Alana Fox, if I knew Tori Fox. Was the Nitwit truly so thick that he had not made the connection between Tori and me?

"Yes, we've met," I said, as calmly as I could.

The Nitwit truly was that thick. He only heard me confirm that I was familiar with Tori. He neither heard the acid tone in my voice nor noticed the look on Jorjana's face. He was as focused on his new idea as that Labrador would have been on a thrown ball.

"Great. So, Tori has some good ideas for the dinner tonight. Go ahead, Tori. Tell them what you told me last night."

Tori beamed at Ken. She straightened up and thrust her breasts forward—an ex-cheerleader move meant to reward men for adoring her. Ken and the head Brat were mesmerized. Jorjana and I, not so much.

Tori knew her audience. She delivered her good ideas directly to Ken and the Brat.

"Last night at dinner, I said that Ken should maximize his exposure while he's in town. I can get another two hundred or so people over here tonight, and Ken could really meet all the heavy hitters in town."

I looked out the glass windows behind Tori. There, just past the pool, stood a tent covering twenty-five tables, each set with ten place settings, one for each guest who had been invited via an engraved invitation over a month ago. The RSVPs had returned via the US Postal Service, and they sat in a nicely stacked deck in front of Jorjana.

I decided the best tactic to battle this catastrophic display of bad manners was to just ignore it. I turned to Ken.

"So, Ken, how do you and Tori know each other?"

"Graham introduced us." Tori answered like I was talking to her. She tried for a casual tone, but she just couldn't keep the smug out of her voice.

"Graham?" I asked like I had no idea who she meant. I knew damn well who Graham was—Malibu's most elusive gazillionaire and one of the few people in town that neither Jorjana nor I knew.

"Graham Tuttle," Tori said, still smug.

"Oh, of course. How do you know Graham?"

I said this as if I, too, knew Graham.

"Let me explain," Ken said.

Thank God. I just couldn't listen to Tori anymore.

"Graham Tuttle and my father-in-law went to Stanford together back in the day," Ken said. "Graham is an old family friend, and he met Alan through some commercial real estate deals. When Graham heard I would be in town for Jorjana's dinner, he introduced me to Alan. Graham figured, correctly, that Alan and I would hit it off."

Alan is my ex-husband. (The Alan/Alana jokes wore thin about ten minutes into our marriage.) Ken's story of Alan meeting Graham Tuttle through commercial real estate, while plausible, was unlikely. Alan got our commercial real estate business when we divorced, but I still sat on his board of directors, and I would have heard if he had met Graham Tuttle along the way. And I hadn't heard a thing. Something was amiss.

"Well, isn't that interesting," I said. I tucked my hair behind my ear. This told Jorjana to just go along with anything I came up with.

"I wasn't aware you and Alan were on the guest list," I said to Tori. I picked the RSVP list off the table. I made a great show of reading it.

"It's not that many people. Just two hundred or so," Tori said.

"Two hundred?"

"Or so."

"Let me get this straight," I said. "You want to bring an extra two hundred…or so…guests to a catered sit-down dinner that you were not invited to? And you are demanding this of the hostess on the day of the event?"

"Is that a problem?" This from Ken.

I was now completely sympathetic to Jorjana's previous frustrations.

"Yes, Ken, there is a problem," I said. "We have a catered event scheduled for two hundred and fifty people for tonight. We can *not* add another two hundred...*or so*...guests at this late hour."

Ken looked confused. Tori looked triumphant. I will admit to being both pissed off and confused.

"You see, Ken, this is exactly what I was telling you," Tori said. "In today's world, you have to be able to react and change quickly. I could send out one text and have *five* hundred people turn up with just a few hours' notice. It's just a matter of knowing the right people and having the right sponsor for the party. I have the friends, and I know the sponsors."

"That's awesome!" The head Brat was impressed. The other Brats stopped typing long enough to look up. "Who're your sponsors?"

Tori picked up her phone. "Let's just say I have a vodka company that owes me a favor or two."

The Brats practically fell over themselves with that news.

"Awesome!"

"There's enough space in here for an epic party!"

"Is it Grey Goose? I bet it's Grey Goose! Ya think Kate Hudson will come?"

Tori's smug little smile grew a bit bigger.

Jorjana put the speculation to rest without raising her voice or landing a punch. She simply raised her hand, and the room fell silent.

"Thank you, Tori, for your insights on an alternative method for introducing Ken to the voters of Malibu. But as you can see, the plans are set for tonight's dinner."

Jorjana pointed to the tent. Tori, Ken, and the Brats all looked outside. The twenty-five tables of ten sported white linen tablecloths. Servers bustled about, laying sterling silver flatware and placing crystal goblets just so. A small stage was decorated with bunting, and a poster proclaimed "Wheeler for Governor." Chandeliers hung from the tent rafters.

"Perhaps you and Alan could host an additional event for Ken at *another time*." Jorjana looked at Tori the way the school principal looks at the kid who threw water balloons at recess. "I will host this dinner tonight in *my home* for *my* invited guests and *without* sponsors. I am certain you understand."

Jorjana's message was clear. No hordes invited via text. No sponsors setting up booths and offering vodka shots served out of bimbos' navels. Her house, her party. Tori had the decency to look admonished.

The Nitwit found a loophole.

"Maybe Tori and Alan could come tonight? I'd like Tori to see how you do things, Jorjana. Then her event could be different. You have room for two more guests, don't you?"

I knew how tightly the tables were set. Tori and Alan would have to sit on milk crates outside the kitchen. Which was fine with me.

"Make that four more," Tori said as she consulted her phone. "Graham and Jack Jessup are coming, too."

The smug was back. I'd like to say it didn't bother me, but it did.

Jorjana reached over and took my hand. There was no secret code in that move. I think she wanted to keep me in my chair.

"Four guests, then," Jorjana said. "But not one more."

"Fine." Tori stood up and gathered her notepad and pencil. "What time should we be here?"

"Five o'clock."

Tori didn't laugh, but it was clear she wanted to. "Five o'clock? Who did you invite? Every old geezer in town?"

"Not to worry—Alan knows everyone. He can introduce you." This from me. Yes, I was snotty.

That took the smug off her face. She left without so much as a good-bye or a "thank you for including me at this late hour and without a proper invitation." I did get some satisfaction in noticing she had put on some weight.

Ken waited until her fat ass exited the Dining Hall. Then he turned to Jorjana.

"We have a problem."

Chapter Three

"You bet we have a problem, Ken!"

I didn't shout. I get points for that.

"What the hell were you thinking bringing Tori Fox here?"

A little louder this time. The Brats dove back into their laptops like ground squirrels escaping a hawk.

"She said I should maximize my exposure while I was in town. I brought her along so we could work out the details with Jorjana. It seemed like such a good idea the way she explained it."

Ken looked like a kid who didn't understand why it was a bad idea to play baseball in front of a greenhouse.

"You do know that Tori is married to my ex-husband, don't you?" I asked, just to confirm my suspicions about how thick the Nitwit was.

I all but saw the light bulb go off over his head. He honestly had not made the connection between Alan Fox, Tori Fox, and Alana Fox—thereby solidifying my assessment.

"No, I didn't know. Is that going to be a problem?"

I looked at Jorjana. She shook her head. I closed my eyes and sighed. Ten years of my life dedicated to keeping Little Miss Tight Buns out of my social circle and one idiot politician blows it all to hell.

"Yes, it's a problem. Besides the fact that Tori and Alan and I *never* socialize, the tables are set. Finding a place to seat four more people is going to be a nightmare."

The Brats raised their heads, no doubt wondering which of them would get the boot from the dinner.

"I will speak with Perry," Jorjana said. Diplomatic as always.

"How did you meet Alan?" I asked Ken. "And don't give me that crap about Graham and Alan doing business together. I would've heard about it."

"But that's what Graham told me," Ken said. "He said he met Alan through a business deal. He thought Alan and I had a lot in common, so he introduced us."

"When did you meet Alan?"

"Last night. Graham and I had dinner at their house. They have a really nice place above Zuma Beach. Do you know it?"

"Yes."

I knew it very well, since I designed the place and supervised its building before surrendering it in the divorce.

"Did your wife attend as well?" Jorjana asked.

"No, Lara doesn't fly in until this afternoon," Ken said.

Well, that explained a lot. The Nitwit was running around Malibu unsupervised and fell into bad company, aka Tori. Who didn't bother to point out that Alan was my ex-husband but then wrangled an invite to the meeting with Jorjana.

I hated to admit it, but it was a smooth move—something I would have done myself.

"We will manage the seating for the dinner," Jorjana said. "But there must be no further additions to the guest list. There will be just the four?"

"Yes, Tori, Alan, Graham, and Jack Jessup."

"Who is Jack Jessup?" Jorjana asked.

"He's Graham's attorney. Graham never goes anywhere without him," Ken said.

"Except to dinner last night," I said.

"Oh no, Jack was there," Ken said. "Didn't I say that?"

My head started to throb at that point.

"You mentioned a problem," Jorjana said. "What is it that concerns you, Ken?"

"I didn't know that Graham was coming tonight." Ken didn't look all that happy about it. "Graham is building my platform on immigration, and he is adamant about sticking to the law. Forgive me for asking, Jorjana, but are all of your household staff legal workers?"

Jorjana stiffened as if he had slapped her. She recovered beautifully, of course.

"I can confirm that for you immediately," she said. She turned to a small table next to her wheelchair. A tray held an assortment of small bells. She picked up a little silver bell and gave it a shake. Perhaps a bit more forcefully than was necessary.

The York staff was trained to respond to the bells. The house was wired so the sound of a ringing bell could be heard in every room. A glass tinkle summoned the downstairs staff; a brass bell brought Perry, her social secretary. The little silver bell was for Caroline, the household manager.

Caroline appeared in an instant.

"Mr. Wheeler is concerned about the legal status of the household staff," Jorjana said. "Will you reassure him, please?"

Caroline was nothing if not well trained. She came to the York Estate via a hoity-toity butler-training school in England. She dressed impeccably in pencil skirts and tailored blouses and wore just the lightest of lipsticks. She was even-tempered at all times. This was amazing, considering the high jinks that she had witnessed over the years—often from me.

"Our household staff are all legally documented workers, Mr. Wheeler," Caroline said. "I can produce the papers if you need them"

"Just knowing you have them is enough for me," Ken replied.

"Thank you, Caroline," Jorjana said. "Would you please inform Perry that we have four additional guests for the dinner. I will speak with him momentarily about the seating arrangements."

Caroline took her leave. She exited out the glass doors leading to the pool. On the other side of the pool was an entrance to the kitchen. As Caroline approached the doors, Perry opened them. Caroline put her fingers to her lips and pushed Perry back inside. The fallout from Tori's invasion had begun.

"Jorjana, I'm sorry to put you on the spot like that," Ken said. "Graham is a stickler about not hiring illegals. He would have my hide if he found out an illegal immigrant was working here."

"I understand. But you have nothing to fear," Jorjana said. She wore her perfect hostess face—the one she put on when she was displeased with a guest's behavior but was too polite to say so directly.

"Is there anything else we should know?" I asked.

I just needed to clarify that Ken wasn't going to bring a wheelbarrow full of monkeys for the evening entertainment.

"I think that's...oh! Here's Spencer!" Ken said.

Into the Dining Hall walked a younger version of Ken Wheeler. He looked to be in his early twenties. He was tall, like Ken, and he kept his eyes on his cell phone. By his side was an older version of the Bunyans out front. Same black T-shirt. Same military-grade haircut. But he carried a briefcase instead of a gun.

"And Mac." Ken sounded less excited to see Mac.

"We are ready to secure the perimeter, Mr. Wheeler," Mac said.

"Come meet Alana Fox first," Ken said.

The kid took his eyes off his phone long enough to shake my hand.

"I'm Spencer," he said. "Pleased to meet you."

"Spencer is our oldest boy," Ken said. "He set aside his senior year at college to help out his dear old dad."

"Where do you go to school?" I asked the kid.

"UOP," Spencer replied, referring to the University of the Pacific in Stockton.

"Good school," I said. "Do you play basketball?"

It seemed like an innocent enough question. Ken Wheeler had captained the Stanford basketball team in his college days. Spencer was certainly tall enough for the sport. He had to be six foot five. But apparently I'd struck a nerve. Spencer shook his head and stared back at his phone. Ken gave an embarrassed chuckle.

"No, Spencer is our swimmer," Ken said. "His brothers play ball for Stanford, though."

And in a nutshell, Ken summed up his family dynamics. I didn't need to see the red flush rising on Spencer's neck to know that he was the black sheep of the family. Not only had he chosen the wrong school, he wimped out on the family sport. I wondered if his year off from school had anything to do with gaining his father's respect. I silently wished the kid luck.

"And this is Mac McDonald," Ken said. "Mac is Graham's security guy."

Mac met my outstretched hand with a handshake intended to bring the recipient to his or her knees. I had anticipated this, however, and I gave back as hard as I got. I thought I caught a flash of surprise in Mac's face.

"My guys and I will keep everyone safe tonight," Mac told me.

"I'm sure Rusty is happy to have your help," I said pointedly. Rusty is the head of Jorjana's security. I couldn't wait to find out what he thought about the Bunyans in the black T-shirts.

"Rusty and I are working well together, I can assure you, Mrs. Fox," Mac McDonald said.

"Well, I think we have covered everything," Ken said. "Is there anything else, Jorjana?"

"As we discussed, you will be busy circulating during the dinner, so my chef will have a meal ready for you and your family at four o'clock," Jorjana said. "I will join you in the kitchen then."

"Yes, of course, and it is much appreciated," Ken said. "Is there anything else I should know?"

I released the brakes on Jorjana's wheelchair. I turned to Ken as we left. "Don't screw this up."

I couldn't help myself.

Chapter Four

"Ken didn't ask if he could bring Tori, did he?"

"No, he did not."

I delivered Jorjana to her suite of rooms on the second floor. I set the brakes on the wheelchair in front of a window that looked west over the Pacific. I placed a knitted throw over her legs. I found a tray of bells and rang the ceramic one that summoned a nurse.

"So tell me what happened."

Jorjana appeared to shrink into her chair. The meeting had drained her.

A nurse arrived with a glass of water and a few pills. Jorjana washed the pills right down. She dismissed the nurse with a nod.

"I expected to meet with Luke and perhaps an assistant. The plans for dinner are well set; there was very little to discuss. You can imagine my surprise when Luke arrived with a dozen assistants and said Ken had new ideas for the dinner. Before Luke could explain, Ken arrived with Tori in tow. And then Mr. McDonald arrived with Spencer and announced an urgent need to discuss security. The meeting was in chaos from the start. Thank goodness Perry was there. He escorted Mr. McDonald and Spencer to see Rusty. At my request, Perry called you. I felt...well, honestly, I felt ambushed. I managed to divert Ken's attention by asking him to practice his speech until you arrived. Thank you for coming, Alana. I am quite beside myself at the moment."

Jorjana York had been a mere baby when her mother died. Her childhood was spent following her father from one diplomatic post to another. Many diplomats send their children to boarding school to lend some measure of structure to their young lives. But

Jorjana's father kept her with him, educated her privately, and showed her a world that few of us could even imagine. She had shared with me the highlights and dangers of living in palaces with gold faucets and nannies who carried machine guns. It had given her a depth of empathy like I had never seen in anyone else. It had also given her a very distinct manner of speaking—a formal dialect that forced people to pay attention to her.

Tall and athletic, with thick, dark hair that had just the right amount of curl, she had been the toast of several continents in her youth. She spoke several languages, knew the difference between a fish fork and a cake fork at twenty paces, and could bluff her way out of any poker hand put in front of her. The only thing that could faze her was bad manners.

She dealt with that in spades when Tori showed up demanding to hijack Jorjana's dinner party.

I had about two minutes before Jorjana went down for a nap. There wasn't time to rehash the entire meeting at length. I decided to skip everything regarding Tori and her ridiculous plans. Jorjana entertained the old-fashioned way—with mailed invitations, plenty of notice, and no photographers. The fact that so many folks thought that kind of party was extinct showed you how well she kept her festivities private. LMTB, with her text invites and vodka sponsors, may have been all the rage, but Jorjana hosted elegant gatherings to which people coveted an invitation. The key ingredient was elegance—something the text-invite-and-vodka-shot crowd would never understand.

There were other matters to discuss.

"What did you think about Ken asking if the staff were all legal workers?"

"I suppose he is within his rights to ask," Jorjana sighed. "But his timing does leave something to be desired. I am quite concerned with his disorganization. He is like a hummingbird—flitting around from one idea to another with no apparent plan. Today's meeting does magnify my worry. And I was not aware that he knew Graham Tuttle."

I fussed with the throw on her legs.

"That surprised me, too. I wonder why Ken didn't ask Graham to introduce him to folks in Malibu."

"Graham Tuttle's circle of confidantes, while influential, is very small," Jorjana said. "He knows few, if any, people in Malibu. Or in Los Angeles, for that matter."

"He could get more people up to that house of his faster than Tori could with her stupid texts. Who would turn down an invite to Graham Tuttle's place?"

Graham Tuttle lived in a secured fortress deep within the Santa Monica Mountains. Everyone in town knew where the place was, but hardly anyone had actually seen it. Rumors abounded, of course.

"Perhaps," Jorjana said. "But you are assuming that Graham Tuttle would welcome a crowd into his home. I believe he has well earned his reputation for being something of a recluse."

"No kidding. How long have we tried to meet the guy?"

Jorjana chuckled. "Years. And then Tori, of all people, will bring him to a dinner here."

I didn't see the humor in it. But then, Jorjana was a better person than I.

"By the way, Alana, I spoke with Lara Wheeler this morning and asked her to meet privately with me this afternoon. My original intent was to discuss my concerns with her about the organization of the campaign. Now that Tori is part of the picture, I have additional concerns. I would like your input as well. Will you join us here at three p.m.?"

"I'll be here," I said.

Jorjana yawned. She closed and opened her eyes slowly as the meds kicked in.

"One last thing," I said. "Where are you going to seat everyone, now that we have to make room for Tori?"

Jorjana reached for her bells. She rang the little brass one.

"The seating arrangement can be adjusted. I will speak with Perry."

I rang a bell for the nurse. I promised Jorjana that I would return at three to meet Lara Wheeler.

Perry and the nurse arrived just as I was leaving.

The Main House is two stories tall and U-shaped. On the second floor, the East Wing houses Franklin York's suite and several guest bedrooms. The second-floor West Wing consists of Jorjana's suite and the rooms for her nursing staff. There is also a physical therapy room and a small kitchen. The South Wing connects the other two and has more guest suites and the office for Rusty, the head of security.

I opened the door to Rusty's office. I had a few questions that only he could answer.

I found him with his feet up on his desk, keeping an eye on a dozen screens feeding video of the property.

"What can I do for ya, Alana?"

Rusty was in his late forties, a thick stump of a man with red hair and freckles. Ex-military cop, father of four, a solid guy.

I pointed to the screen that showed the Bunyans in the black T-shirts at the front door.

"Guns? Really? Jorjana would have a fit if she knew."

Rusty took his feet down. He pointed a remote at the screen. The camera focused in on the Bunyans.

"Yeah, I know. It's ridiculous. Mac McDonald was in here this morning trying to make a case for armed guards tonight. I told him what he could do with his goons and his guns."

"What's with this sudden need for security? Ken isn't even the party nominee yet."

"Mac works for Graham Tuttle, and he's got a lot invested in Wheeler's campaign. Apparently there have been threats to Wheeler. So Mac and his guys have orders to guard the guy like he is the governor already."

"What threats?"

Rusty paused. He looked back at the screens. The Bunyans were walking around the Escalades like they were guarding the entrance to a prison.

"Mac wouldn't say."

"Don't you think this is a bit much? Can't you and your guys handle this?"

"Look, the private-security world is a small one. I know Mac pretty well. He's got a plum job up there working for Tuttle, but he has to do what his boss says, just like I have to follow Mrs. York's rules. So Mac and I worked out a deal. His guys and their guns will walk the perimeter tonight and keep Graham Tuttle happy. My guys will watch over the house and keep Mrs. York happy."

"Mac agreed to that?"

"Yeah. Funny thing about that, though. I didn't get the impression that Mac thought the threats were all that urgent. He didn't press me when I said my guys would take the house. If Mac thought Wheeler was in real danger, he would have insisted that his guys were placed inside."

"And he didn't."

"No. It's not for lack of manpower, either. Tuttle keeps a small army out at his place, all decked out with those black shirts and pants like guerillas."

"Why?"

Rusty shrugged. "Who knows? Those billionaires can be crazy bastards."

"Graham is coming to the dinner tonight," I said.

"Really?" Rusty was surprised. "Mac didn't mention that."

"What if Graham Tuttle doesn't like the arrangement that you and Mac agreed to?"

"He can go have dinner somewhere else, then."

I left Rusty and made my way downstairs and out to the porte cochere to fetch my car.

Imagine my delight to find Ken standing just outside.

"I thought you would have left by now," I said by way of suggestion.

"Mac and Spencer are touring the property to make sure everything is in order," Ken said. "I'm just waiting for them to get back."

"You could be here awhile," I said.

"Yeah, this place is huge."

That it was.

I hoped this exchange would end our chitchat. But then the valet drove up in my car.

"This is your car, Alana?" Ken could not have been more surprised if the valet had arrived in a coach-and-four. He pocketed his phone and walked to the car—a 1966 Ford Mustang.

In a cruel twist of fate, when Alan and I divorced, I got his collection of vintage cars—all twelve of them. It never ceased to amuse me how differently men reacted to each car. The '48 Jaguar convertible appealed to lawyers, the cherry-red '56 Thunderbird drew the eyes of musicians. The 1952 Porsche convertible attracted gay guys like seagulls to an unsupervised sandwich. I suspected the cause of that attraction is that I painted the Porsche hot-pink.

I did this just to annoy Alan when Tori was expecting their first kid.

The Mustang was the one car all men seemed to love equally. Personally, I didn't get it. The car was painted the most god-awful color of sinus-infection-yellow. It stood out next to the fleet of Escalades like a bumblebee on a black tile.

"Is that the original paint job?" Ken circled the car, studying the rims of the tires, stroking the upholstery. He stopped on the passenger side. "Look! It has the High Country Special medallion! You can tell it's a '66 'cause there's no date!"

The valet ran around to get a look. Even the Bunyans stopped pacing long enough to take a gander. Ken pointed to the medallion, and they all admired it for a lot longer than I felt was necessary.

"This was Ford's first limited-edition Mustang," Ken said to the valet. "It was a special promotion for the Colorado dealers. The '67s and '68s have the date on the medallions. These Mustangs only came in three colors, Columbine Blue, Timberline Green, and this one, Aspen Gold. I like the gold best, myself."

The valet agreed the gold was great. But then, he was a member of the well-trained and properly documented York staff. If Ken had said the car would look better painted purple with green side-walls, the kid would have agreed.

I knew where this was going. The valet was on the clock; the kid would stand there all day and listen to Ken go on and on about the amazing history of the Ford Mustang and how America was a better place because of it. Ken did seem to know his car history pretty well. I, however, had things to do, and I needed the damn car to do them.

Ken popped the trunk, the better to discuss how spacious it was. Which it was. I figured there was room for at least one politician, one valet, and two Bunyans.

While Ken and the valet leaned over the trunk, a movement in the distance caught my eye. A footpath from the Main House wound behind the Carriage House and down to the fruit orchard. I spotted Perry, the social secretary, and three women trotting along the path. They weren't running, but they weren't stopping to smell the roses either.

Perry saw me and put his fingers to his lips. And then led the women out of sight. All three women were wearing the Estate day-time uniform. All three were Hispanic. Fortunately, Ken was too engrossed with the Mustang to witness the exodus.

Perhaps Caroline had not been entirely truthful about the documentation on the York staff. My opinion of her rose a few notches.

"Dad! Is that a '66?"

Spencer raced up the drive, Mac hot on his heels and two more Bunyans bringing up the rear.

"Yeah. What do you think, Spencer?"

Seriously, you would have thought the Mustang was a long-lost relative.

"This is exactly like the one you had," Spencer said. He hopped in the driver's seat and ran his hands over the steering wheel.

"It sure looks like it, doesn't it?" Ken agreed. He took another lap around the car. Mac and the Bunyans nodded their approval.

"This is a beautiful car, Alana," Ken said. "Are you interested in selling it?"

Spencer got out of the front seat without taking his eyes off the car.

I took this opportunity to hop in.

"I might be," I said. "Let's get this dinner over with, and we can talk about it."

I put the car in gear.

I did gun the engine as I went. All the better to drive up the price.

Chapter Five

FRED (THE CALABASAS GARAGE)

Wes Field was anxious as all get-out.

"Fred, I'm telling ya, it's an epidemic! Cars are disappearing like someone is beaming them up into the sky!"

Fred Winthrop lifted his head from under the hood of the 1952 Porsche he was tinkering with.

"Beaming them up? C'mon, Wes."

Fred wiped his hands on the shop towel tucked into the pocket of his coveralls. He closed the hood and gently wiped his fingerprints off the car's hot-pink body. He groaned as he straightened. At six foot six, it was a long stretch down for Fred to reach the Porsche's engine. It hadn't always been a tough move, but then he hadn't always been sixty-three years old, either.

He stepped back and regarded the Porsche the way a proud parent watches over a favored child.

"She's a beaut, Fred," Wes said. "Too bad Alana had her painted pink. You shoulda talked her out of it."

"I tried, but you know how Alana can be."

"Yeah, but painting a car a stupid color just because her ex-husband had a kid is crazy."

Fred agreed, but he would never say that out loud. There were plenty of days when Fred really hated the fact that Alana had ended up with the twelve cars in the Fox Collection. Mr. Fox would never have defaced the cars. On the other hand, Alana paid

Fred very well and provided him with a place to live. And, repainting aside, she let him care for the cars as he saw fit. Before the divorce, Mr. Fox had been all over his case about every minor ping or rattle. In Fred's opinion, an engine that was over fifty years old was entitled to a groan or two.

Nine years earlier, the '52 Porsche had suffered from rust and had been in real need of a paint job. Fred had suggested a creamy white—a classy color, in step with the history of the car. But Alana had been so pissed at her ex-husband she had the car painted hot-pink. Something about thinking the new Mrs. Fox was having a baby girl, and the hot-pink car would be a reminder every time Mr. Fox passed it on the road. As luck would have it, that baby turned out to be a boy.

Women.

Fred and Wes stood in the warehouse where the cars of the Fox Collection were stored. The floors were coated with an epoxy finish that Fred kept as clean as he kept his dinnerware. The service lift was as shiny as a new dime. Fred's tool chests were locked in place around the lift, ready to go whenever a car needed attention. The warehouse was located in Calabasas, just outside the Malibu city limits.

In one corner sat a 1956 MG, which now sported turquoise body paint and orange flames, the victim of the new Mrs. Fox having Baby Number Two. Next to it was the 1954 Chevy truck painted candy-apple red in honor of Baby Number Three. Actually, Fred had never been that fond of the truck's original spearmint-green color, so the new paint was an improvement in his opinion. But he did worry about which car would be sacrificed if the new Mrs. Fox decided to pop out Baby Number Four. The other nine cars in the Collection were in mint condition. Repainting any one of them would drastically reduce its value.

Rich people.

"Want some coffee, Wes?"

"Don't mind if I do. Can I pull the 'Vette in first?"

Wes's Silver Anniversary Corvette was parked just outside the bay doors of the warehouse. The 'Vette was his pride and joy. He often stated that he intended to be buried in it.

"Sure, pull her in, and I'll lock the doors."

Wes sprinted out the bay doors. Wes was as thin as Fred was tall. He moved like a jackrabbit—quick and all over the place. He hopped into the Corvette and turned the engine just enough to let out an explosive *vroom*. Then he slowly drove into the warehouse and parked next to a red 1948 Jaguar XK-120.

Fred was particularly fond of that Jag. If Alana got it into her head to repaint that car, well, Fred wasn't sure just how he might react. He hadn't taken early retirement from the Postal Service because he was such a calm and patient guy.

The two men climbed the wooden stairs leading to Fred's apartment above the warehouse. The space was small, just a sitting area, a compact kitchen, and a bathroom across from an alcove that held the bed. But Fred liked it. He didn't need to store a lot of stuff—his wardrobe consisted of seven sets of navy coveralls and one marrying-and-burying suit. He owned four pairs of work boots and one pair of dress shoes. The best part of the apartment was that it boasted a lot of wall space.

"Have a seat, Wes. The coffee will be done in a minute."

Fred turned on an electric kettle to heat the water and pulled a French press coffee maker from a cupboard. He put coffee beans through an electric grinder and added them to the pot. When the water boiled, he poured it over the ground beans. While it steeped, he put two bone china cups and saucers on a sterling silver tray with a creamer of milk and a bowl of sugar cubes. He loaded a plate with biscotti. He put small spoons onto linen napkins and pressed the plunger on the pot. He carried the tray to the coffee table in front of the couch. Wes smiled.

"You run the best coffeehouse in SoCal, Fred!"

"I don't need much, but what I need, I need to be good. Have one of these biscotti. I just made them last night."

The two sat in silence, enjoying the coffee, the cookies, and the artwork that covered every inch of the walls. Ornate frames housed colorful images of women with bobbed hair staring into wishing wells, horse-drawn wagons laden with hay, folksy scenes of children drooling over apple pies, wallpaper samples from the arts and crafts era, black-and-white sketches from the art deco era, and one lone shadow box holding a signed baseball.

"You sure got a lot of stuff hanging up on the walls, Fred," Wes said as he finished his coffee. "Any of it worth anything?"

"It's worth whatever anyone will pay me for it," Fred said. "But it doesn't matter. I'm not selling. I collect it because I like it."

"That's how I feel about my 'Vette. I get people asking me all the time how much I want for her. But I'm not selling her. I'm keeping her until I die."

Wes paused.

"Unless someone steals her from me. I'm telling ya, Fred, cars are just up and disappearing."

"What exactly are you hearing?"

"Out in the Central Valley, there's a lot of cars gone missing. Mostly muscle cars, but anything that runs fast seems game. Word is a gang is getting them to the port in Stockton and shippin' 'em out with new VINs and paperwork. And they're sending 'em to Asia, so that's the last anyone will ever see of 'em."

"That's been going on forever. What's different now?"

"It's the sheer number. I mean, dozens and dozens of cars in the last couple of months. My friend in Stockton says he thinks someone at the port is in on it. I think he's right. Ya hear about stolen cars shipping out of Long Beach all the time, but not dozens of 'em. And never out of Stockton."

Fred got up and walked to a small desk that held his computer. He typed in a few words, and a web page popped up.

"What's that?" Wes looked over Fred's shoulder at the computer screen.

"It's a web page a buddy of mine runs to keep up with what's going on in the car world. Ya know, sales and values and scams. He's pretty well connected to the cops, too. OK, this is interesting."

"What is it? I don't have my glasses with me."

Fred took a moment to read the article.

"My buddy says that the increase in stolen vehicles happened right after Jesus Rodriquez was released from prison. Remember Rodriquez?"

"Who could forget? He ran that gang out of San Jose. Those guys practically stripped the Bay Area of muscle cars."

"Until he got busted, remember? My buddy says Rodriquez is picking up where he left off, now that he's out."

"Why don't the cops bust him again?"

"They have to catch him first." Fred closed the web page and started typing.

"Yeah, well, the cops should try harder," Wes said. "At the rate things are going, they're going to run out of cars to steal in NorCal and head down our way. I'm looking into a tracking device for the 'Vette. You got any leads on a good system?"

Fred didn't answer. He was reading a newspaper article from the *Sacramento Bee* dated ten years earlier. Wes squinted at the screen.

"What's that? Reviews on tracking devices?"

"No, something much more interesting."

"You gonna give me advice on a tracking system or not? I don't have all day."

Fred copied the article, pasted it into an e-mail, and pushed "send." Then he turned the computer off and grabbed a set of keys from a pegboard by the door.

"I'll show you what I was thinking about putting in the Jag. It's a GPS system that you can access from your computer or your phone."

"Why haven't you installed it?"

"I guess I didn't want to admit that I really needed to."
"But I convinced you that you need to?"
Fred thought about the article from the *Bee*.
"Sure, Wes, I'll give you the credit. Thanks, buddy."

Chapter Six

Downtown Malibu consists of a cluster of strip malls that line up on either side of PCH. Paparazzi shots of celebrities are usually taken around there. The local glitterati flock to the Starbucks at the corner of Cross Creek Road and PCH and are swarmed by the paparazzi as they order their lattes. The celebs wishing more exposure wander over to the Malibu Country Mart for a local, sustainable salad from John's Garden while their kiddies frolic in a playground under the shadow of a giant sculpture that looks like a hammer. The paparazzi circle freely while the celebs chow down at outdoor picnic tables. I swear every movie studio in LA has a clause in their contracts that actors must wander about Malibu before their movies come out.

Suffice it to say, the Country Mart can feel like the center of a tornado as scruffy paparazzi chase even scruffier celebrities. And by chase, I mean, plowing over anyone standing between them and the money shot.

A quieter alternative for regular folks needing caffeine is found at the Malibu Town Center. Tucked behind the Country Mart, the Town Center has a locally owned coffee shop that roasts its own beans. The place boasts the original name of Beans.

My office is located in the Town Center. As I pulled into the parking lot, I could smell the latest batch of roasted beans. I set the parking brake and gathered my things just as a mass of stringy-haired paparazzi swarmed out of nowhere and surrounded my car. They raised cameras outfitted with oversized lenses, looking like a SWAT team armed with bazookas. The shutters on the cameras clicked so fast and loud that it sounded like rounds of rifle fire.

Then they saw it was just me, and they scattered. Except for one.

"What are you guys doing over here?" I asked him.

"There's nobody at Starbucks," he said. "We all came over to Beans for coffee and saw the car and thought you were somebody."

"You can keep tabs on every minor celebrity in town, and you can't remember which cars I drive?"

The guy shrugged and fiddled with a device in his hand. It looked a lot like the contraptions used to play video games, but it was outfitted with a small screen.

Just then something whizzed past my head. At first I thought it was a seagull. But it hovered overhead and made a whirring sound. I looked up. The whirring thing was about the size of a shoebox with propellers on top.

"What's that?" I watched it fly away.

The guy laughed as he fiddled with his contraption.

"It's my new drone. I can take shots from just about anywhere now. Look."

He turned the screen toward me. There was a photo of me looking up.

"This is a good shot of you, Alana. I'll send you a copy. Thanks for the tip on Clooney last week!" And he was gone.

Unlike other Malibuites, I appreciate the paparazzi. They are like flies. Everyone finds flies annoying, but no one thinks about what the flies are up to. They likely see things that no one else does. That kind of information can come in handy to someone like me who likes to know everything. So I toss tidbits to certain paps in exchange for tidbits tossed back to me. Works like a charm.

I wondered how much better my information might get with the use of a drone.

I didn't waste a lot of timing musing about this. I had work to do.

The Malibu Town Center is two stories tall and was built to look like a Spanish Hacienda. The parking lot is where a courtyard might be. The ground floor has retail, and the second floor hads office space. A veranda runs around the outside of the second floor and is accessed by a staircase. I was halfway up the stairs when I spotted Spencer Wheeler.

Spencer was alone as he walked into Beans.

I gave a nanosecond's worth of thought to wondering where Ken Wheeler was, but even that short thought irritated me. I put the Wheelers out of my mind and headed to my office.

My little office consists of a cozy waiting area decorated in shades of gray and ivory, with a few well-placed photos of me partying with the Malibu elite. The outside window is made of frosted glass that lets in light without letting prying eyes (paparazzi) see in. The door leading to my office is also of frosted glass but has a pattern designed to allow me to see who is entering. The space is light, airy, and feminine and is intended to put clients at ease.

I tossed my stuff onto the chair opposite my desk, kicked off my shoes, and settled in to tend to my business. My first order of business was Marjorie Dunham. I'd stopped at the bank and deposited her check, so I was ready to put my plan for her in motion. I pulled my social calendar up on my computer to plot her social engagements. I created a file for her, sent out introductory emails, and brainstormed a list of ideas for her social life. I was on a roll when my phone rang.

The caller was Stan Sanchez, the man in my life.

"Hey, handsome," I said.

"Hey, yourself. You're not driving, are you?"

Stan was a Malibu cop. He had no tolerance for driving while talking, which I had been known to do. In my defense, none of my cars was capable of accommodating cell phone technology. Hell, most of them had manual windows.

"No, I'm in the office. How's your day going?"

"That's why I called. Something's come up with Maddie."

My heart sank. Not today. Not with the dinner tonight.

"What's going on?" I kept my voice as neutral as possible.

Stan was a divorced dad of four (count 'em, four) kids. Something always came up, often with Maddie, the oldest kid, who was fourteen going on twenty-five.

"It's complicated. I'm on my way over to her mother's. If I get tied up, can I just meet you at Jorjana's tonight?"

Stan sounded like he was trying to juggle balls while running backward on a treadmill. I knew that tone. So I did what I always did—pretended that I understood his dilemma.

"Do what you have to do. I just want you to be there. Call me later."

I hung up and tossed my phone onto a low table next to my desk. I kept my phone there because I could see alerts out of the corner of my eye but not distract clients sitting opposite me. I believed this was called good manners.

I stared at the phone. How many times in the last month had Stan called to cancel? Four? Five? I wished the reasons for the cancellations were his crazy work schedule or my crazy social life. But every instance had to do with his kids. One had a broken arm. Another got a bad report card. One of them even managed to get stuck up a tree. With four kids, Stan's emergencies were never-ending. Add the fact that his ex-wife did everything she could think of to keep him away from me, and it was a wonder I ever saw the guy at all.

I did my best to accommodate each crisis. Dinner plans became lunch the next day. A red carpet movie premiere became Netflix at my house. A weekend in Santa Barbara turned into a brunch at Ollo down the street. But lately it seemed like I had to change our plans every time one of his kids stubbed a toe.

I hoped like hell that whatever the latest crisis was, it was wrapped up before 5:00 p.m. I needed his support as much as his kids did.

I didn't get a chance to work myself into a dither. My office door flew open and let in a human hurricane.

"*Darling*! There you *are*! I was beginning to think you were *never* going to come to work today!"

David Currie burst into the room like a paparazzo after a top-less starlet. He plopped down in the client chair.

David is solidly middle-aged, a former rugby player and currently Malibu's dandy-about-town. He also manages Errands, Etc., an errand-running service that operates two doors down from my office. He is my second-best friend, right there after Jorjana.

"I just got back from a meeting at Jorjana's," I told him. "You'll never guess who was there."

I gave David the rundown on Tori's latest appalling behavior.

He was not properly appalled. "Well, darling, it appears that Little Miss has made friends in spite of your efforts."

"That's the best you can do? Tori made friends? What about Tori lying to Ken Wheeler to get herself invited to the York Estate and then trying to hijack Jorjana's dinner? What about Tori acting like she's so high-and-mighty because she's met Graham Tuttle? What about…"

I could have gone on for hours. And normally I would have—with David cheering me on every outrage of the way. But he didn't join in. He didn't even look upset.

"Wait a minute," I said in midrant. "You know something, don't you?"

David wiggled a bit in his seat, the way he does when he has a juicy bit of gossip in his pocket.

"I may have heard a thing or two about Little Miss," David said.

"So tell me."

"Well, darling, now that little Chaucer is in school, Little Miss is the queen of the school moms."

Chaucer was the oldest of Tori's three brats. I did the math. He was probably nine.

"Took her long enough—that kid must be in third grade."

"Second grade. Tori kept him back a year because he's a fast little devil."

I stared at David. I would have understood Greek better.

"Darling, all the savvy mommies keep their little boys back so that when they hit high school, they will be physically ahead of the other little boys. This gives them an advantage in getting an athletic scholarship."

"What does that have to do with Tori?"

"The school moms are competitive, darling." David held his hand up and counted with his fingers. "Tori is a pretty girl. She has a big house with a view. Her husband is loaded. And her boy is a good athlete. Everything a Malibu queen needs."

I didn't question how he knew this. As manager of Errands, Etc., David talked to everyone in town. Even the people I avoided, like LMTB.

"Big deal. She's made friends with the school moms. She has no business hanging around with my friends."

"True, darling, but Little Miss does have to keep her hubby happy."

"What does that mean?"

"I have heard murmurs that your ex is growing weary of the school-age crowd. It seems he would like to play with people his own age."

"Then he should have stayed married to me."

Perhaps I should explain here that after nearly twenty years of marriage to me, Alan Fox developed a desire for children. We married young, so I probably could have produced an heir at age thirty-nine. But I wasn't willing. And LMTB was.

Alan and Tori married the day after our divorce was final. Chaucer arrived ten months later, followed quickly by two more.

"Alan got what he wanted," I said. "He didn't want me, so he and his little wife need to stay out of my life."

"No one would dare cross you, darling," David said. "Tori has nothing to offer your friends."

"Nothing but access to Graham Tuttle. How did that happen?"

"No idea, darling. Perhaps you can ask your ex tonight at the dinner." David thought that was hilarious.

"You're not being very supportive, you know," I said to him.

"Oh, darling, you have nothing to worry about. This is a once only event. Tori will never set foot on the York Estate again. You know Jorjana will prevent that."

"What about Tori's new friend Graham Tuttle?"

"That, my dear, you will have to figure out on your own." David got up. "I have work to do, but I will nose around and see if anyone knows anything about Mr. Tuttle."

"Why don't you change your mind and come tonight?"

"No, darling. I can't afford to appear political in any way. You will be just fine. Now come in early tomorrow and tell me *all* about it—especially what Little Miss was wearing!"

And with that he swept out the door.

In his wake I heard him say, "She's just in there. *Oh, Alana!* You have a little visitor!"

Into my office walked a young teenage girl. She had dark hair worn in one long braid. She wore a school uniform with the shirt partially tucked in and the skirt rolled up. Not as short as I used to roll my skirts up, but short enough to turn heads. She had a book bag hefted on one shoulder. She was cute, I suppose. And she reminded me of somebody.

Partly defiant, partly terrified, she looked at me and said, "Are you the lady that's screwing my father?"

Chapter Seven

This is why I dislike children so. You just never know when they are going to screw up a day that is already half in the toilet.

I'd never met Stan's kids, but I'd seen pictures. That, and the fact that Stan had just called in a panic over Maddie, led me to deduce that the girl standing in my office was Maddie Sanchez.

Good Lord, could the day get any worse?

"Who are you?" I asked. I was not about to give her the satisfaction of knowing that I knew who she was.

She faltered a bit. "I'm Maddie?"

"Maddie who?" I straightened the papers on my desk. I pulled out the drawer and dropped a pen into it. Then I pulled my phone onto my lap.

"Maddie Sanchez? Ya know, Stan's daughter?"

"Shouldn't you be in school?"

With my left hand, I texted Stan. *Maddie in my ofice. Send smeone to get her.*

OK, so my spelling was off. I'm not left-handed.

Tears welled up in Maddie's eyes. She even went as far as to get her lip to tremble. I made a mental note to suggest to Stan that acting school might be a good investment.

"I...I...I'm not going b-b-back to that f-f-fucking school!"

"Does your mother know you talk like that?"

"I *hate* my mom! Where's my dad?"

"I don't know." Technically that was true.

"I'm not leaving until he gets here!"

"Fine. Have a seat. I have work to do."

She plopped down in the client chair and glared at me. Things were not going the way Maddie had expected. Her fourteen-year-old brain likely had convinced her that showing up unexpectedly in my office would produce rainbows and unicorns and make everyone as happy as a day spent at the mall. When she saw that I really was going to ignore her, tears flowed.

OK, maybe she really was upset. I'm no expert on children.

"Aren't you going to call him?"

"No."

"Wh-why not?"

"You are not my problem."

That really took her aback. She was used to her parents rushing to bail her out of everything.

"But you have to call him. My mom took my phone."

No wonder Stan was so upset. He had no way of contacting his missing kid. I felt a little bad about being annoyed with him.

"How did you get here?" I asked the kid.

"I took the bus."

"From school?"

"I didn't go to school. I went straight to the b-bus."

"Why?"

"Because I *hate* school, and my mom is a bitch!"

Her head went down into her hands, and the sobs shook her whole body. While I agreed with her assessment of her mother, I did worry the tears would stain the upholstery on the client chair. To save myself a cleaning bill, I produced a box of Kleenex.

"Here, catch." I tossed the box to her. "Let me get this straight. You hate your school, and you hate your mother. Am I correct in assuming you and your mom had a big fight?"

A nod of the head and a honking blow of her nose.

"So you hopped on a bus to get away. Why did you come here?"

"B-because I want to live with my d-dad."

Great. I see little enough of Stan as it is.

"Yeah, but he doesn't live here. Why did you come *here*?"

"Because my mom said h-he spends all of his time with you."

"Well, your mother is wrong about that. How did you find my office?"

"I Googled you."

Of course she did.

Just then my office door opened, and two Malibu cops entered. I was familiar with both of them, but no pleasantries were exchanged.

I didn't say they liked me.

"We've come to take you home, Maddie." The cops stood on each side of Maddie and placed gentle but firm hands on her shoulders. "Your parents are worried."

Maddie glared at me as if I had somehow betrayed her. I held up my phone and wiggled it.

"I can text without looking," I said. "Give your mother my regards."

My call to Stan did not elicit the gratitude and high praise I expected.

Stan was angry. "Why did she go to *your* office? How did she get there?"

His tone of voice suggested this was somehow my fault. This did not sit well with me. I had felt sorry for him and everything.

"I didn't lure her over here, Stan. Maybe you should ask her mother."

"There are a lot of things I need to ask her mother. Obviously there are problems that I don't even know about. How did she look?"

"She's fine. And so am I, by the way. But I've got a pile of work to do, and I've wasted enough time dealing with your kid. You're welcome."

I hung up. And I didn't pick up when he called back.

Chapter Eight

I am not entirely heartless. My parents divorced when I was young, so I understood Maddie's pain. But just because I understood did not mean I intended to get involved.

I didn't like being a child. I didn't want one of my own. And I sure as hell didn't want someone else's kid. Even if she was Stan's daughter.

Don't think that I am taking the easy way out. Not wanting children is a complicated calling.

If someone said to me, "Alana, you really should become a neurosurgeon," and I answered, "No, thank you, I don't want to," the topic would go away. But stating that you do not want children seems to compel society to try to change your mind.

My life would have been a lot simpler if I had just procreated. My husband would never have divorced me. I would still live in a beautiful house above Zuma Beach. People would not whisper behind my back, "She never had children, you know," and then shake their heads in pity.

I was never willing to give up life in a fully adult world and abandon the business I loved in order to care for a child.

Ironically, the business went to Alan in the divorce. My choice to be child free left me husband free and business free as well. So I built a new business all of my own. Which I was proud to say was thriving. But it needed my attention to continue to do so.

I pulled up my social calendar on the computer with every intention of returning to work. After ten minutes I admitted defeat. Between the nonsense of dealing with Tori and the drama of Maddie Sanchez, I was beat.

I rallied enough to send the most urgent emails and then shut down for the day. I locked up my office and headed for home.

Home is a two-story, two- bedroom, mock-Tuscan villa-ette right smack-dab on the sand on Malibu Beach Road. The address isn't as prestigious as the Malibu Colony, but my little abode could nab me a cool six mil if I ever choose to sell.

The house boasts a one-car garage. This is a desirable feature in a town where so many million-dollar beachfront houses have no garage at all. And I am grateful that I can park a car in a locked structure adjacent to my house. My other eleven cars are garaged in a warehouse in Calabasas. I have a guy who lives in a studio apartment above the warehouse and tends to the cars. He shuttles the cars back and forth as I need them. He keeps the cars running as well as they can run, fills them with gas, and washes them with all the love and attention they deserve.

The guy's name is Fred.

Fred was standing in front of my garage when I returned home. Next to him was parked my hot-pink 1952 Porsche.

Fred Winthrop is a polar bear of a man. Pale skin, white hair, arctic blue eyes, as tall and wide as an igloo, he used to deliver the mail in Malibu. When he retired from the Postal Service he presented himself at our front door and requested the job of caring for the cars he saw my husband driving around town. Alan hired him on the spot.

I got Fred in the divorce.

Fred was dressed in his usual uniform of navy-blue coveralls and leather work boots. I didn't recall requesting delivery of the Porsche. It was unlike Fred to show up unannounced.

I pulled the Mustang into the garage.

"Hi, Fred. What brings you over?"

"I had to pick up some stuff in Santa Monica, and the Porsche needed a run. I stopped by to see how the Mustang is doing. You want me to take it and leave you the Porsche?"

Fred is nothing if not a doting caretaker to my cars. He is happiest when I rotate them daily, as he likes to put as few miles on them as possible. He hates it when I have the cars repainted. He does know I only do this when Alan and Little Miss Tight Buns have a baby. I readily admit I do this to annoy Alan. Fred does not see the humor in it.

"I think I will hang on to the Mustang for another day or two, Fred. By the way, do you have any idea what it's worth?"

You would have thought I had asked how to turn the car in for scrap metal. Fred moved to position himself between the Mustang and me.

"Why?" His nostrils actually flared as he replied.

"Jorjana's hosting a dinner tonight for Ken Wheeler. You may have heard of him—he's running for governor. Anyway, he asked if I was interested in selling. He seems to know a lot about Mustangs."

Fred walked into the garage and circled the Mustang in much the same way Ken Wheeler had—taking in every detail, noticing everything. I seriously don't get what it is about that car. The color is just awful. Bad enough that I almost wish Alan and LMTB would have another kid so I would have an excuse to paint the Mustang.

"It needs a wash. Are you home for a while? I can wash it and return it in a couple of hours."

"Sure, thanks. I need to be at Jorjana's by three."

I handed the keys to him and went in search of a bubble bath, forgetting entirely that he never told me what the car was worth.

Chapter Nine

FRED

Fred pulled the Mustang out of Alana's one-car garage and parked it on the street in front of the house. Then he pulled the Porsche into the garage, grabbed his toolbox, and lowered the door. Back in the Mustang, he pulled out onto Malibu Beach Road and headed south.

Alana's beach house was located about midway down Malibu Beach Road. From the street, the house didn't look like much. Which made it less likely that a car thief would target her house. Unless, of course, they followed Alana and her car home. That possibility had crossed Fred's mind in the past, but he hadn't felt compelled to act on it.

His conversation with Wes and the article in the *Bee* convinced him it was time.

Fred drove to the end of the street, made a left, and then turned right into the corner gas station. He parked in front of the service bay, where he found the station owner fixing a flat.

"Hey, Doug! Mind if I do a quick project in the other bay?"

"Hey, Fred! Go right ahead. Want a water or anything?"

Fred declined the water and pulled the Mustang into the bay. He popped the hood, grabbed his toolbox, and set to work.

A half hour later, the Mustang was outfitted with a GPS tracking device. It wasn't state of the art, but it would allow Fred to sleep at night. Once the Mustang was back in the Calabasas warehouse, he would install a more sophisticated tracker—one that was more likely to fool professional car thieves like the gang picking the Central Valley clean.

Fred cleaned the windows and vacuumed out the interior- the new SoCal car wash thanks to the drought- and spent a few minutes shooting the breeze with Doug. Then he drove back to Alana's and switched the cars again. As he hung the key to the Mustang on a hook in the garage, he realized just how lax the security was in Alana's garage. Anyone could bust down the flimsy door, and there would be the keys just hanging in plain sight.

He made a mental note to discuss it with her as soon as possible. Then he closed the garage door. He climbed back in the Porsche by stepping over the door and shimmying his way down into the seat. Then he made a mental note to try once again to fix the damn door. He tried not to look foolish as he drove the hot-pink convertible back to Calabasas.

Chapter Ten

By two o'clock I was bathed, napped, dressed, and ready for a drink. I made my way downstairs to the kitchen and threw together my favorite cocktail: gin, limoncello, and diet ginger ale over ice. I call it The Usual, and it cures whatever ails me. The gin calms my nerves; the ginger ale soothes my stomach. And the limoncello prevents the possibility of scurvy.

I took the drink out to the back deck and sat myself down for a good think.

My oceanfront deck is the largest room in my house—five hundred square feet of Saltillo tile and teak patio furniture. It has a tendency to disappear into the Pacific Ocean when a storm hits it just right. But California's drought has kept storms at bay, so the deck was in solid shape, for a change.

An umbrella over the dining table provided shade, so I sat there and pondered the ocean. Which goes to show you how out of sync I felt. I do not like to ponder the ocean. I find the constant pounding of the waves on the beach to be depressing. I prefer to view the ocean from a good distance. Say, from a house on a hill overlooking Zuma Beach. The very house where Little Miss Tight Buns was likely dressing for dinner. In a dressing room with Murano glass chandeliers and a velvet couch with a view of the ocean. At a distance.

I took a sip of my drink. Ten years spent keeping LMTB out of my social circle, yet she would dine that evening at the York Estate. The anger I'd eased with a bubble bath rose again. I took another sip in hopes of dousing it.

She would waltz in with my ex-husband in tow and...And what? I checked the anger long enough to consider what would actually happen when LMTB did arrive at the dinner.

She would arrive, dressed inappropriately no doubt, with Alan on her arm. She would know no one. Alan, however, would know everyone and be forced to introduce his second wife to people he had not socialized with since he was married to me. I felt my mood lighten. I knew how Jorjana's and my friends would react. They would be polite and then suddenly need to refill a drink. Or go to the loo. Or simply walk away. Tori may have bluffed her way into the dinner, but the odds were good that she would not feel welcome.

If life had taught me anything, it was self-preservation. My mother checked herself daily into a bottle of Carlo Rossi Chablis after my father left us. Therefore, I learned, at age ten, how to get myself to school and cook dinner. I got myself a full-ride scholarship to college. I found a trust fund attached to a decent guy and married him at nineteen. I built a wildly successful commercial real estate business out of the trust fund. And when the decent guy lost his mind and left me, I made damn certain he paid for it. Alan Fox's desire for a family life costs him $750,000 a year and a seat on his board of directors.

My sense of self-preservation (and the stiff drink) forced me to admit that my desire to embarrass LMTB was petty. It was a fun thought, but it was petty. And petty behavior could harm me. So, as entertaining as humiliating Tori might be, it was better for me to take the high road. I would simply ignore her, and my friends would take my lead. Tomorrow Tori would return to the mommy life and be out of my life. My spirits rose again.

But there was the puzzle that was Tori's relationship with Graham Tuttle. Assuming there was one at all. What "business deal" had Alan done with the reclusive billionaire? Alan was not the world's best businessman. His board of directors told him what to do lest he screw up the entire operation. No one had mentioned a new deal at the last board meeting. I knew enough about Graham Tuttle to know the man was shrewd. What interest did he have in a commercial real estate business? With any luck, I could chat him up at dinner. Jorjana would certainly seat the man at our table.

I tossed back the rest of my drink. I felt calmer than I had all day. It was time to go.

I arrived at the gate of the York Estate precisely at three o'clock. Outside the gate stood two of Mac McDonald's Bunyans dressed in black T-shirts. No guns this time, but they each held leashes hooked to German shepherd dogs. Inside the gate stood two of the York Estate security guys. No dogs there. I presented my invitation to one of the Bunyans, while the other one checked under my car with a mirror attached to a long handle. I was cleared to enter. The York guys gave me a wave as I drove by.

As I drove up the hill, I caught glimpses of more Bunyans walking dogs around the perimeter of the property. It appeared that a small army of black-clad men was crawling around the place. Graham Tuttle's payroll likely rivaled a small country's GDP.

I pulled up to the porte cochere and handed the car off to a valet. Flanking the front door were two York security guys. Dressed in navy polo shirts and khaki slacks, each of them had an earpiece in his ear. No guns.

"Good afternoon, Mrs. Fox," one of them said. "Caroline asked for you to find her before joining Mrs. York."

"Do you know where she is?" I asked.

"Try the kitchen."

The kitchen is located at the far end of the house. To get there I walked through the West Reception Hall and past a series of hallways that led to and fro. The York Estate employs dozens of people who access the house through the hallways. I found it odd, therefore, to walk all the way from the front door to the kitchen without encountering a single soul.

The York kitchen has two separate preparation areas. The smaller side features a cozy breakfast nook that seats twelve and looks out over the herb garden. An additional bunch of folks can sit at the island, which is not quite big enough to hold a square dance. A ten-burner gas range, two dishwashers, a walk-in fridge, and a pantry with a view of the garden made up the rest of the small kitchen.

Next to the pantry is a rustic barn door that opens to the catering kitchen. This is where things get big. The catering kitchen was designed to cook for five hundred. You could land a plane on the stainless steel counters. There are three gas ranges, three prep sinks, a giant kettle the size of a Jacuzzi, steam ovens, convection ovens, and a commercial dishwashing apparatus. The pantry has its own zip code. An automated door leads out to the backyard and allows servers to come and go with ease.

I found Caroline in the catering kitchen with her arms folded, while the caterer yelled into his phone.

Tony Buswell had been hired to cater the dinner. Tony was well known to anyone who had ever thrown an elegant affair in Malibu, which was just about anyone I knew and certainly everyone on the guest list for the dinner. He charged a flipping fortune but knew every current food issue of everyone in town. For this alone, he was worth the extra bucks. It went without saying that he was also organized. Which, apparently, was not the case at the moment.

"Where the hell are the greens for the salad?" Tony held his phone to his ear like he was trying to stop blood flow. "A truck? Whaddya mean a truck? Do you know how backed up PCH is gonna be in an hour?"

He paced around the stainless steel counter, his face as red as the tomato sauce simmering on the stove.

"What's going on?" I asked Caroline.

"Someone forgot to load the greens for the salad onto the catering truck," Caroline replied. "Tony only just noticed."

"Can't we just run down to the grocery store and buy some?" I asked.

"He called the store. They don't have enough for two hundred and fifty people."

"How far is the truck coming?" I asked.

"Santa Monica."

I looked at my watch. It was 3:15 p.m. With a little luck, the truck had a chance of making it to Malibu in time to serve salads by six o'clock. But it was cutting it close.

Tony slammed his phone on the counter.

"You!" He pointed his finger at someone behind me.

I turned to see one of the York cooks cowering behind a prep sink.

"Are those lemon trees out there?" Tony pointed to the garden.

The cook nodded.

"Go out there and pick a few dozen lemons and slice 'em real thin. Then make a batch of chicken stock. Enough for two hundred and fifty. If the greens don't get here, we'll give 'em consommé with a lemon slice to start."

The cook ran off. Tony turned to Caroline.

"You got enough soup bowls for that?"

"We do," Caroline said. "I will have the bowls brought over. Do you need anything else?"

"I need to fire somebody is what I need," Tony said. "But the bowls will do for now."

Caroline took me by the arm and led me to the China Room.

The China Room was one of the spaces off the warren of hallways and was slightly smaller than a basketball court. Racks of stainless steel shelving were lined up like soldiers in formation. Each row of shelving was labeled to identify which china pattern was stored there. The plates and cups and bowls were packed in quilted boxes to protect them from dust. The floors were specially made of soft linoleum. The shelves had deep lips on the edges, and the racks were bolted to the floor. In the event of an earthquake, it was probably the safest room in the house.

It was not like Caroline to draw me aside, much less pull me away into a room. Even before she spoke, I felt a knot growing in my stomach.

"Mrs. Fox, I am so glad you are here. We have a problem. Mr. Tuttle's request that tonight's staff all be of legal status has left us quite shorthanded."

I remembered seeing Perry escort three women away from the house earlier in the day.

"We have only two members of the evening staff on duty," Caroline said. "And with Perry gone, I must supervise the dinner party, which leaves the upstairs unsupervised. We still need to prepare for the Wheeler family to stay the night."

I was confused. Not over the missing staff. Of course the York Estate employed immigrants—who else would dust the mantelpieces and change the sheets? What this had to do with Perry, I had no idea. Perry was a fair-skinned social secretary. He was about as Mexican as I was.

Caroline sensed my confusion. "Perry is Canadian."

"So?"

"His immigration papers are not entirely in order."

"What immigration papers? He's Canadian."

"And Canada is a foreign country."

Well, hit me upside the head with a maple leaf. Who knew a Canadian could be an illegal immigrant?

I may be thickheaded when it comes to immigration issues, but I figured Caroline wanted my help.

"What do you need me to do?"

"Do you know anyone with a clear head who can supervise the upstairs staff until the dinner is over?"

The York Estate is not unlike a hotel. The ground floor is the public area. Upstairs are the private areas that include Jorjana and Franklin's suites. Not to mention the guest suites and, the private dining and lounging areas. The upstairs staff includes four nurses, two physical therapists, two chefs, a butler for Franklin, and a small army of maids. Given Jorjana's fragile health and Franklin's fragile state of mind, there are dozens of people working around the clock.

Caroline oversaw everyone, but there was an evening house manager for the night shift. The evening manager's name, of course, was Carlos. Under normal circumstances, Carlos would see the suites were ready to welcome the Wheeler family, while Perry would supervise the party downstairs. Caroline would have the evening off. With Perry and Carlos gone, no wonder Caroline was stressed. Fortunately, I knew just whom to call.

"I'll get hold of David Currie," I said. "He can supervise upstairs."

Caroline visibly relaxed. "Thank you, Mrs. Fox. Mr. Currie is the perfect solution. He won't mind?"

"He will do anything for Jorjana." Which was true.

I left Caroline to count out two hundred and fifty consommé bowls, found a cozy chair in the West Reception Hall, and dialed David.

"Darling! Do you have some juicy tidbits for me already?"

"Yes and no. Listen…" I gave him the rundown and assured him that he could stay out of sight.

"But you need to get up here before the guests arrive," I said.

"I'm on my way."

That settled, I called Rusty and made sure David could get past the nonsense at the gate.

I passed Caroline in the hallway just as the sound of pots hitting the floor came from the direction of the kitchen.

She gave me two thumbs up. I wasn't sure I believed her.

Chapter Eleven

I was late for my introduction to Lara Wheeler. I sprinted up the stairs to the second floor. I paused at the top to catch my breath. Then I headed to Jorjana's rooms in the West Wing.

After losing their daughter, Jorjana and Franklin found it impossible to share a bedroom. Jorjana frequently awakened in pain and needed medication. Franklin rarely slept at all. When designing the Main House, they agreed to separate rooms. This did not mean they were apart. You only needed to see them together to understand their devotion to each other.

Unfortunately, Franklin was around less and less. Tonight's dinner was another event that he would miss due to his latest need to shoot things. Jorjana had mentioned something about elk in Alaska.

I found Jorjana in her lounge area. She was dressed for dinner in a red silk dress with full sleeves. She wore gold sandals and gold hoop earrings. Her hair was loose and fell in tumbles of curls around her shoulders. When I entered, she arched her eyebrow as if asking a question. She wanted to know how things were going downstairs. I gave her a nod to let her know all was under control. We were far enough away from the kitchen that she wouldn't have heard the crashing pots and pans, and I saw no reason to alarm her.

Jorjana sat at a table set with tea. Her wheelchair was out of sight. She was not alone.

Lara Wheeler sat across from Jorjana. She had the kind of blond hair that cost a fortune to look that natural, a flawless complexion that was no less costly to maintain, and perfectly manicured nails.

She wore a simple sleeveless navy dress that showed off her upper arms and paid tribute to whoever her trainer was. Plain gold wedding band, gold watch, and pearl earrings.

Something about her posture suggested she knew how to sit properly in an English saddle.

"Alana! Allow me to introduce Lara Wheeler," Jorjana said.

Lara Wheeler rose to shake my hand. She was tall—the kind of tall in a woman that takes you aback. No wonder she married a former basketball player.

"Alana, it is a pleasure to meet you," Lara said.

"The pleasure is mine," I replied. "Are Ken and the boys here too?"

"They will be here shortly," Lara said as she retook her seat. "Jorjana arranged for us to eat as a family beforehand. Ken and I rarely have time to eat at these things, so we end up stopping at In-N-Out for a burger around midnight. It's delicious but not so great for my waistline!"

We all laughed. Lara was obviously a pro at lighthearted chit-chat. I wondered how often she used that story to break the ice.

"Alana, please sit. May I pour you some tea?" This from Jorjana, going into her nurturing mode.

Before I took my seat, something whizzed by an open window behind Jorjana. It looked like something Wile E. Coyote would make to catch the Road Runner.

I peered out the window to confirm my suspicions. Sure enough, it was a drone. Just like the one the paparazzo had used to take my picture that morning.

The drone disappeared over the bluff.

"Is something wrong, Alana?" Jorjana asked.

"No, everything is fine," I said. I cranked the window open a bit more. "I just wanted a little more air."

As I turned around I pulled my phone out of my pocket. I pretended to shut it off while actually sending a text to Rusty

Winston. *Drone just flew by.* I didn't need to tell him where I was. He knew.

"Jorjana tells me that Ken has been a bit scattered," Lara said as I took my seat. "I do appreciate all that you two have done to help keep him in line."

She shook her head with a smile, like we were talking about the shenanigans of a little boy.

"Are there any more changes we should know about?" I asked more curtly than was necessary. "I understand that Graham Tuttle is now attending."

"Graham is coming?" Lara was surprised.

I gave her the abridged version of the story. I didn't get into the discussion over illegal domestic help.

"Forgive me," Lara said. "Ken didn't mention this to me."

The silence that followed lasted just long enough for Lara to recover her public face.

"I have advice to offer," Jorjana said to Lara. "I feel there is a weakness in the lines of communication within Ken's campaign staff. I have witnessed confusion within the ranks on more than one occasion. I do have experience in correcting this very problem."

Lara didn't answer right away. I sensed she was assessing her options.

"Jorjana, you have hit the nail on the head," Lara said finally. "Ken can be forgetful. We are reaching a point in the campaign where we do need to tighten our communication. As a matter of fact, Ken and I are having a working dinner tomorrow night at Graham's home. There are others attending who also have advice for the campaign. I would love for you to attend if you are available."

Jorjana was delighted. "Thank you, Lara, nothing would please me more."

No kidding. If Jorjana added Graham Tuttle to her Rolodex, she would have access to pretty much everyone who mattered in the entire universe. While she and Lara worked out the details,

I started to wonder who really was driving the "Wheeler for Governor" bus. Was it Graham Tuttle, Lara, or, God forbid, Ken Wheeler himself?

"How long has Graham been involved in the campaign?" I asked Lara.

"Graham is an old friend of my family," Lara said. "He and Pops tossed around the idea of Ken running for office for years. But Graham has only been actively involved in the last couple of months. Why do you ask?"

"Just curious."

I took a moment to reassess Lara Wheeler. She was polished, no doubt. With her simple hairstyle, clothing, and jewelry, she could be a walking ad for WASP Inc. She was articulate. She was Stanford educated, so she was no dummy.

Ken's disorganization must drive her nuts, I thought. I wondered if Lara hoped that Graham could keep Ken focused. Then I remembered that Ken had apologized for Graham's demands about "illegals." It didn't sound to me like Ken Wheeler and Graham Tuttle were on the same page. But that hadn't stopped Ken from laying down Graham's rules.

"Ken threw us a curveball this morning," I said. "He insisted that all the servers tonight be legal workers. He said it was Graham's idea."

Lara kept her public face on, but I could tell she was not happy to hear this. I suspected there would be a very interesting discussion in the Yorks' guest suite that evening.

"I did not know this, either. Jorjana, I am truly sorry that you were put in that position."

"There is no need to apologize, Lara," Jorjana responded. "My household manager assures me that our staff tonight are legally cleared to work in the United States."

Jorjana caught my eye and winked.

I never got around to dissecting LMTB and her awfulness. One of Jorjana's legally documented maids appeared.

"Mrs. York, Caroline says that Mr. Wheeler and his sons have arrived."

"Thank you, Maria," Jorjana said. "Shall we join them?"

While Lara and Jorjana made their way to the elevator, I dropped in to make sure Rusty had received my text about the drone. I found him at his desk frowning at the camera feeds.

"We're on it."

I had no doubt.

I heard Ken's voice in the entryway as I left Rusty's office. I wasn't ready to deal with him yet, so I took the back stairs to the kitchen. It appeared that things had calmed down since I left. Tony had stopped yelling, and the cook was stirring a large pot of chicken stock. A pile of freshly sliced lemons smelled delicious.

"I think the greens will get here on time," Tony said.

"Either way, you're covered," I said. "I just had a meeting with Jorjana and Mrs. Wheeler. Did anyone tell you that all your servers have to be legal?"

"Yeah, I went through all that with Caroline. No worries. It isn't pilot season yet, so I've got starving actors working tonight."

"None of them are Canadian, are they?"

He didn't get a chance to answer. Just then a drone dropped out of the sky and hovered outside the kitchen window. Then it spun around and flew away.

"Did you see that?" I was startled.

The caterer shrugged. "That's the latest paparazzi toy. Those drones can get in anywhere. Who's coming tonight that they'd be interested in?"

I had to think about that. Truly there were no celebrities on the invite list. "No one that the gossip sites would even know."

"No worries, then. The drone will watch the cars arrive, and once they realize there are no celebrities, they'll fly off to another event. Ya kinda have to give the paps credit. They can fly those drones from almost anywhere and not have to race all over town to get photos."

I should have taken more note of his comments, but I was distracted by a text message.

It was Stan. *I'm on my way, but I've got Maddie with me. Can you set a place for her?*

What the hell? What else could possibly go wrong?

Chapter Twelve

The Wheeler family was gathered around the table in the small kitchen by the time I finished with Tony. The whole family could be a Ralph Lauren ad. The boys had their mother's blond hair and their father's good looks. They were a press agent's dream.

If I had to guess, I would say the boys' mother had dressed them. All three wore gray slacks, a long-sleeved cotton shirt with one button undone, and loafers. I don't know much about kids, but I suspect young adult males wouldn't dress like that unless under the threat of severe repercussions.

Jorjana sat to the side and watched the boys tear into a platter of fried chicken with a bemused expression on her face. Or was it horror? The boys attacked the chicken like coyotes after a kill.

"Alana, come and meet our boys!" This from Ken.

To my surprise, all three boys put down their chicken, wiped their hands on their napkins and stood to greet me.

"Boys, this is Mrs. Fox. Alana, you met Spencer this morning; he's our eldest. This is Todd, who's a junior at Stanford. And Evan is a freshman."

I shook each boy's hand and told them to resume eating. I took a seat next to Jorjana. The York cook delivered an ice-cold glass of Chardonnay for me. As he placed the glass on the table, he whispered in my ear, "Mr. Currie has arrived. He said to tell you not to worry."

I nodded my thanks and took a longer draw on the Chardonnay than was probably necessary.

"Spencer hasn't stopped talking about the Mustang all day," Ken said.

"I'd love to take it for a test drive, if you really are interested in selling it," Spencer said as he reached for more chicken.

"I haven't decided one way or the other," I replied.

"It's definitely worth more than you paid for it," Spencer said. "How long ago did you buy it?"

"I didn't buy it. My ex-husband had it when we met."

"Which was how long ago?"

That was none of the kid's damn business. My irritation must have showed. Spencer flashed a smile meant to disarm me. A regular chip off his mother's block.

"I don't mean to pry. It's just a car's value can go up if there has only been one owner, or if the car has remained in one family. Just take that into consideration when you set a price."

"Alana will be well advised when the time comes," Jorjana said. "Her garage is run by a man very knowledgeable about vintage automobiles."

"You have more cars?" Ken sounded surprised. The boys stopped chewing long enough to look up. Even Lara seemed impressed by this.

"Well, yes. I have twelve altogether, and I have a guy who takes care of them."

"What do you have?" Spencer asked,

You would think I would know this off the top of my head, but I did have to stop to remember. After all, it was not my collection originally. Now if you asked me how many square feet of travertine tile went into that house above Zuma Beach, I could tell you in my sleep.

I managed to reel the list of cars off without calling Fred to confirm.

"You have a twelve-car garage in Malibu?" Spencer asked. "You must have quite the acreage."

I winced. The twelve-car garage was attached to the house with eight thousand square feet of travertine.

"No, I have a garage in Calabasas. Fred shuttles the cars back and forth for me as I need them."

"Who's Fred?" Spencer was quite the Curious George.

"Fred Winthrop. He takes care of the cars for me. I don't know the first thing about changing oil."

"Who does anymore?" Lara said. "Boys, it's getting close to starting time. Go freshen up. And review your notes."

The boys all looked longingly at the apple pie on the counter.

"We will have dessert together after the guests have left. Now go."

All three boys neatly folded their napkins on the table and stood up. Without prompting, they thanked the cook for the dinner and Jorjana for having them.

"It was my pleasure," Jorjana said. "If you will excuse me, I must touch base with Caroline. Spencer, will you please assist me?"

Spencer wheeled Jorjana out of the kitchen, his brothers in tow. Which left me alone with Ken and Lara.

I didn't waste anytime. I had something to get off my chest and I didn't want Jorjana to hear what I had to say.

"Let me make something clear," I said to Ken. "This dinner is meant to introduce you to people that you would never meet without Jorjana's help. You will be charming. You will listen to what the guests have to say. You will not embarrass Jorjana. Do you understand?"

Ken blinked. He obviously was not used to being talked to like he was four years old. But I had his and Lara's attention, so I went on.

"Every single person on the Estate tonight is in the country legally, and they are all bending over backward to make this night a success. So go out there and be charming. And remember this—Jorjana has gone to a lot of trouble and expense to put this dinner on for you."

And just in case he didn't hear me the first time, I added, "Don't screw it up."

Chapter Thirteen

The festivities started promptly at 5:00 p.m.

The valets moved cars with an efficiency rarely seen outside an operating room. Jorjana and Ken waited at the front door and greeted everyone as they arrived. The men wore collared shirts, which in Malibu is practically black tie. The women wore dresses that cost more than their face-lifts. They all declared that they were thrilled to see one another.

As I expected, Tori arrived with Alan in tow and dressed in a rumpled shift that looked like a brown paper bag. The thing hung loose on her, accentuating her weight gain. Alan looked as lost as a kid in a corn maze, as per usual when he didn't have a proper adult to show him what to do. I ignored them both.

Waiters circulated with trays of champagne. Four fully stocked bars offered harder libations. A second wave of waiters provided small nongluten, vegan bites for those who actually ate in public. The drought delivered splendid weather. Tony emerged from the kitchen, caught my eye, and held up a bag of salad greens like they were gold medals.

Lara and her boys circulated in pairs, thanking each guest for coming. I had to admit they were good at it. Lara and Spencer broke the ice, and Todd and Evan followed with the cute factor. The Head Brat kept Lara and the boys moving along.

The evening had all the makings of a lovely Jorjana York soiree.

And then Graham Tuttle sauntered in.

It takes a lot to impress the Malibu crowd. Keep in mind these folks run into celebrities at the gas station, the grocery store, and the vet's office. They live and surf elbow to elbow with gazillionaires. Presidents and despots sunbathe on their beaches. So the average Malibu resident is somewhat jaded when it comes to encountering the rich and famous. A lot of that has to do with the fact that the rich and famous often share too many details about their lives. It's hard to be curious about someone who has posted pictures of her bikini wax online.

Graham Tuttle, however, was a different sort of rich and famous. He maintained an air of mystery. And in Malibu, that is as rare as cellulite.

Midseventies and fit, Graham looked every inch the gazillionaire. He wore a dark suit, white shirt, and no tie. The watch on his wrist cost as much as my beach house. But no amount of money could restore his hairline. Graham Tuttle sported a comb-over that fooled no one. Well, maybe it fooled him. You would think the man could afford a mirror.

Graham was not alone. At his side was a guy who could not have been more obvious if he had the word "lawyer" tattooed on his forehead. Behind them stood two guys dressed in black T-shirts and black cargo pants. They had had the decency to leave their guns elsewhere. The four men stood stock-still and surveyed the East Reception Hall.

Jorjana's guests did their damnedest to appear nonchalant, but the cocktail chatter faded to whispers. I wouldn't say the crowd stared, but a herd of dragons could have cavorted in the pool, and no one would have noticed. One woman opened a compact and pretended to check her lipstick while staring at Graham Tuttle in her rear view. Several men pretended to brush lint off the back of their slacks and stared at Graham Tuttle as they turned. Only the wait staff kept moving—offering champagne and tiny bites to a crowd no longer interested in free booze and gluten-free food.

The whispers and stares lasted mere seconds. Then speculation roared up, and the crowd went giddy.

"I didn't know this guy knew Graham Tuttle. Did you?"

"I wasn't sure Graham Tuttle was actually real."

"Who knows him? I need to pitch an investment idea to him."

"I wonder where he's sitting?"

I overheard this last comment and wondered that myself.

I went in search of Caroline. I found her in the tent surveying the set tables.

"Graham Tuttle just showed up with a guy who looks like his lawyer," I said. "Where is Jorjana seating them?"

Caroline stood next to Table One—the table where Jorjana was to be seated, along with Stan and me. One look at Caroline, and I knew that had changed.

"Jorjana has them at her table," Caroline said. "I had to move you and Mr. Sanchez to the assistant's table.

The assistant's table was something Jorjana always set up but placed off to the side. It was a place to stash unexpected guests— usually someone's personal assistant. I'd planned on putting Maddie Sanchez there, just to get her out of the way. Now I could look forward to actually dining with her.

Great. Just great.

"Fine," I sighed. "Stan's daughter is coming, too. Her name is Maddie."

"I had to put Mr. and Mrs. Fox at that table as well," Caroline said.

I can only imagine the look I gave her.

"Mrs. York said you would understand," Caroline explained as she took a step backward. "She did not want the other Mrs. Fox seated at Table One. Under the circumstances, she did not want to reward Mrs. Fox for her behavior."

I hated to admit the seating made sense. The last thing I wanted was for Tori to sit next to Graham Tuttle in front of everyone of importance in Malibu. Actually the last thing I wanted was to dine with Tori, Alan, and Maddie Sanchez, but I had no choice.

Caroline quickly changed the subject. "Is Ms. Sanchez allergic to anything?"

"She's allergic to behaving. She'll get along great with Tori," I said as I left.

I found Graham Tuttle and company belly up to a bar, the crowd warily circling around them. No one had yet summoned up the courage to introduce himself or herself. It occurred to me that approaching Graham first and having everyone think that he already knew me could only improve my credibility as Malibu's most connected resident.

"I'm Alana Fox." I put out my hand in greeting. "Jorjana and I are delighted that you could join us."

Graham Tuttle ignored my hand, but he did introduce me to the other guy. I made it look like I expected this.

"This is Jack Jessup. He's my lawyer."

Jack Jessup was older than me but younger than Graham. I put him in his midsixties. He was the kind of guy who would fade into the background, and you would never know he had been there. But I knew what he did. Jessup kept Graham Tuttle's name out of the limelight. Given how little anyone knew about Graham, the lawyer did his job damn well.

"I'm pleased to meet you, Jack," I said.

Jessup took my hand, but his attention was focused behind me.

I turned to find Lara and Spencer approaching.

"Good evening, Graham," Lara said. "I was surprised to hear that you were joining us. And you've brought Jack, I see."

It was subtle, but Lara managed to convey her displeasure that she was not told about Graham and Jessup showing up. Graham gave the smallest of nods but did not appear distressed at her disapproval. I wondered if Jorjana knew what she was getting herself into by offering to help these people out.

"Good evening, Lara." Jessup exchanged air kisses with her. To Spencer he said, "Hello, Spencer. Staying out of trouble?"

"Yes, sir," Spencer said as his face reddened.

"Good to hear, good to hear. Now let's go find your dad."

And off Jessup went in search of Ken. Spencer followed like Jessup was taking him to spend an evening watching paint dry.

Lara and Graham watched them go.

"He's not a bad kid, Lara," Graham said.

This time Lara shot a glare at him that made Graham take a step back. The two guys in the black T-shirts moved, but Graham raised his hand, and the T-shirts stopped.

I never found out what that was all about.

Stan and Maddie chose that moment to show up.

I left Lara and Graham facing each other like two gunfighters at the OK Corral.

Stan and Maddie looked adorable if you like that sweet father-daughter thing. Stan has dark hair and dark blue eyes. He's fit, and the jacket he wore enhanced his broad chest, even if it wasn't the one I'd bought him. He's not bad looking, either—- my heart leaps up every time I see him. He wore a blue shirt that matched his eyes.

Maddie wore her long hair down and had flat-ironed it straight. It hung to her waist, and she held it back with a blue ribbon. Her blue dress matched her father's shirt. She wore ballet flats, and she looked as happy to see me as I was to see her.

"Hey there." I gave Stan a kiss that was a little longer than it needed to be. "Hi, Maddie. Glad to see you're OK."

She ignored me.

"Maddie, what do you have to say to Alana?" Stan prompted.

"Thank you for having me," Maddie mumbled.

"And what else?" Stan again.

"Sorry for interrupting your day."

I looked at my watch. It was 5:44 p.m. There wasn't time to explain to Stan who our dinner companions would be. It served him right for almost being late.

At 5:45 p.m., dinner bells chimed, and Jorjana and Ken led the crowd into the tent. By some miracle, by 6:00 p.m. sharp, the guests were seated. The sun had set. The view over the bluff showed lights blinking at the Country Mart and in the windows of the homes up the hills. There was no wind. The temperature was perfect. Tea candles sparkled on the tables.

Maddie, Stan, and I sat at the assistant's table in that order. The table was situated better than it deserved to be. I suspected Jorjana had the thing moved out of Siberia and within spitting distance of the tent. The evening could have been tolerable, all things considered. And then Tori and Alan showed up.

Tori was displeased with the seat assignment. Caroline seated them so Tori's back was to the stage. She did have a dead-on view of Stan, which most women would have enjoyed. But Tori did not appreciate it. She plopped down in a huff.

Alan, bless his little heart, had better manners. He reached across the table to shake hands with Stan.

"Alan Fox. This is my wife, Tori."

Stan, being a cop, was used to thinking fast on his feet. He rose to shake Stan's hand. "Stan Sanchez. This is my daughter Maddie."

Both men looked at me like the seating arrangements were my fault. I ignored them and signaled a waiter to pour more Chardonnay.

The lights in the tent dimmed, and the guests hushed. A spotlight shone on a raised platform. Above the platform hung a "Wheeler for Governor" poster.

Ken Wheeler pushed Jorjana's chair up a short ramp to the platform. Ken handed a microphone to her and stepped away. She smiled at him in that way that she has. She addressed the crowd so that everyone felt she was speaking just to them.

"Thank you for finding time to join us this evening," Jorjana said. "I am so very happy to introduce Ken Wheeler to you. I met Ken last year and was impressed with his insight into the problems we face in California. I believe that he would be an excellent governor, and it is my hope that you will agree. I am pleased to introduce to you California's next governor, Mr. Ken Wheeler."

Applause, smiles, and warm, fuzzy feelings abounded as Ken wheeled Jorjana down from the platform. Truth be told, the warm feelings were more likely due to the generous wine pours than Jorjana's introduction. But either way, by the time Ken took the stage, the guests were plenty relaxed.

I gave Ken this. He didn't screw up. He properly thanked Jorjana for hosting and the guests for coming. He gave the short version of where he came from and where he saw the state going. The crowd divided their attention between listening to Ken and craning their necks to see what Graham Tuttle was doing.

Graham kept his eyes on Ken but leaned toward Jack Jessup through the whole speech. He whispered to Jack after each of Ken's major points. Jessup took notes on his phone. The T-shirts stood off to the side.

Ken wrapped it up by introducing his wife and boys. He explained that he and Lara and the boys would circulate while everyone enjoyed their dinners.

"Not to worry about us, though," Ken said. "Jorjana made sure we were well fed before everyone got here."

This brought about the intended laugh. And signaled the wait staff to serve the salad course.

To serve twenty-five tables of ten and one table of five, you need an army of legally documented wait staff. Fifty servers, each balancing five plates, descended on the tent and laid the salads just as Ken started chatting with his first table. The Head Brat hovered next to Ken, with his eyes on his watch. Lara and Spencer took the other side of the room. Evan and Todd started in the middle. It worked like a charm. No table was ever more than one table removed from some member of the Wheeler family. A jazz trio played softly in the background. More servers stood at the ready with wine. I could feel the mood of the room shift toward festive. Everything was going according to plan.

The assistant's table had a nice view of the pool and all of the action under the tent. Luke kept Ken on schedule. Lara and the boys followed suit. Stan took turns talking to me and then to Maddie. I felt myself relax. The dinner was off to a good start.

A waiter swung by with a bottle of wine in each hand. Alan opted for red.

Tori declined. "No, thank you. I'm pregnant."

I heard a gasp. It came from me. I tried to cover it up. "Wow. Four kids now. You'll be busy."

And immediately I made plans to have the Mustang painted any color other than sinus-infection yellow.

Alan disrupted those plans right away. "Actually, five. We're having twins."

I honestly had nothing to say to that. I was so shocked, I couldn't even think of another car to repaint. Stan squeezed my hand under the table. It didn't help.

I distracted myself by studying the salad that had caused so much angst in the kitchen. I had to admit, it was more appetizing than the plan B consommé. It was a lovely combination of arugula, fennel, and peppered strawberries.

"This looks good," Maddie said. "Did you make up the menu, Alana?"

I nipped a snarky comment in the bud. Even in my frazzled state, I could tell that Maddie was making an effort.

"The caterer worked with Jorjana on the menu," I said instead. "It does look good, doesn't it? But it almost didn't happen."

I went on to tell the tale of the missing salad greens. I felt benevolent enough to embellish the story and managed to get a laugh out of Maddie. Alan smiled, too. Tori looked smug.

Just as I was digging into the notorious salad, a woman at the next table grabbed at her throat. She couldn't speak. She seemed to be having trouble breathing. Her husband jumped to his feet and got behind her. He thumped her on the back. She slipped out of her chair onto her hands and knees. And promptly threw up.

"Honey, are you OK?" The husband was on his knees, peering at her face. She nodded, closed her eyes, and threw up again.

Stan was up in a nanosecond, rushing to provide aid.

I got up, expecting to help Stan quietly move the couple inside and summon Jorjana's nurse. I figured the poor thing had choked on something. It would be less embarrassing for her to be tended to away from the party.

Tori got up too.

"I'm a nurse," she said to the woman's husband. "Let me help."

I'd forgotten that LMTB had been a nurse once upon a time. I tend to overlook positive aspects of people I despise. I stepped aside. I'm not that fond of vomit.

Tori turned the woman on her side and took her pulse. Stan supported the woman from behind.

"Take a deep breath," Tori said. She held the woman's head in her hands.

I looked around, hoping to spot Caroline. But she was at the far end of the tent, and I couldn't catch her attention.

Then, suddenly, another guest grabbed at his throat. He, too, fell out of his chair and vomited.

And then another person, and another.

In a matter of seconds, every table had someone in distress. Some grabbed at their throats, some vomited, some stood and waved their arms to summon help. The quiet, contented murmur of a dinner party exploded into screams.

Someone yelled, "We've been poisoned!"

The crowd seemed to rise from the tables in unison.

"Alana, what's happening?" Maddie was at my side, her face white.

"Did you eat the salad?" I grabbed both of her arms, my question racing ahead of my thoughts.

"No."

We both turned toward the tent. The guests were either on their feet or on their knees. The tent smelled of vomit and panic.

"Everyone *stop*! Listen to me!"

Ken Wheeler stood on a chair. He kept his hands up, as if to hold the crowd in place.

"Don't panic. If you feel sick, put your fingers down your throats and force yourselves to vomit."

Ken spoke loudly and calmly, and his voice carried authority like a firefighter carries a fire hose. He kept the monologue going—encouraging the well to help the sick and reassuring all that help was on the way.

"If you feel fine, help the person next to you."

Whether it was his reassurance or the fact that no one else offered a better idea, he kept the crowd from bolting. The stricken vomited with abandon. The well helped the sick. Everyone followed Ken's directions as if he were calling a square dance.

Stan was on his phone, calming but firmly issuing instructions.

"The York Estate. About thirty down. Possible poisoning. Wheeler is not injured. Send everyone you've got."

Tori stayed with the woman on the ground and gave instructions to those around her. She showed the husband how to keep his wife propped up, and then she moved to the next table.

The York staff jumped into action. Caroline sprinted around the pool with a walkie-talkie in one hand and a cell phone in the other. Two of the York nurses ran into the tent, medical bags in hand. Security lights popped on, and the pool area became as bright as noontime. Rusty flew out of the house and into the kitchen via the automatic door. It did not escape my notice that he carried a gun.

In the distance, sirens sounded.

"Alana?" Maddie's voice was tiny but scared. I pushed her toward the kitchen.

We burst through the kitchen door to find Tony and the cook facing a wall with their hands held up high. Rusty stood behind them with a gun pointed at their backs. Half-filled bags of salad greens spilled all over the stainless steel counter. A T-shirt armed with a gun and a German shepherd blocked the door leading to the smaller kitchen.

I put my hands in the air and whispered to Maddie to do the same. For once, she did as she was told.

"I'm just taking this girl to a safe place," I said to everyone who held a gun.

Rusty grunted.

The T-shirt moved to one side.

I hurried Maddie through the door and into the small kitchen. I pulled a chair away from the table and pointed down.

"Get under the table. Stay there until your dad comes to get you."

She crouched under the table. I pushed the chair back in place.

"Don't move. Don't say a word."

I peered under the table. She looked impossibly small, with her arms wrapped around her legs and tears welling up in her eyes. But she nodded. I left her there. I wasn't at all sure I had done the right thing, but some odd instinct told me to stash her out of harm's way. It was all I could think of.

I raced through the staff hallway, past the China Room and into the West Reception Hall. The sirens were closer. Caroline opened all the French doors leading from the house to the pool just as the first round of firemen and medics poured through the front door. There seemed to be a lot of them. The air filled with a crackle of radios.

"We have fifty down. Apparent poisonings."

The York nurses, efficient as always, directed the medics to the sickest patients. Blood pressure cuffs and oxygen masks and portable cots and stethoscopes were put to work. Vital signs were taken. The sick were carted away. Cops were everywhere. It was noisy and chaotic. But Tori's voice rose over the turmoil.

"Somebody get over here! Jorjana isn't breathing!"

And my world came crashing to a halt.

Chapter Fourteen

I made it to Jorjana's side in a nanosecond. As fast as I moved, the paramedics moved faster. A circle of them kept me away from her. I had to jump on a chair to see.

Jorjana looked like she was sleeping. Her hands fell loose at her sides, her eyes were closed, and her head tilted forward. There was vomit all over her lap. But even from my perch on the chair, I could see that she wasn't breathing. Her face was pale. Her lips were blue.

One of the medics put a hand on her neck. He wore a latex glove, a detail I found fascinating. I wondered why anyone would need to wear a glove when touching Jorjana. Then I wondered why the hell it was taking everyone so long to take care of her. Everyone stood watching the guy with the latex glove.

All of this wondering took three long seconds.

"She has a pulse!"

This was the magic phrase. Two men worked together to lift her out of the wheelchair and onto a stretcher lying on the ground. Her head was tilted back and a plastic tube inserted down her throat. The tube was attached to an oxygen tank. She was covered with a blanket. An IV went into her arm. A blood pressure cuff went onto the other arm. One of the medics stated her vital signs out loud.

A firefighter repeated her vital signs into a radio that looked to me like a remote control for a TV. Next to him stood one of Jorjana's nurses, filling in data as needed.

"We have a fifty-nine-year-old female paraplegic not breathing. Pulse is forty. Blood pressure is eighty over forty-five."

I was no doctor, but none of it sounded good. I couldn't take my eyes off Jorjana. She was so still and pale. The tube coming out of her mouth looked hard and cold. There was a small army of medical personnel around her, and yet she did not move. And there was nothing I could do to help her.

My head was spinning. I had the presence of mind to step down off the chair and sit down. I leaned forward and took a few deep breaths as the sounds of rescue continued around me. The clang of metal as a gurney arrived. Commands given and commands repeated. My whispered prayers that Jorjana would be fine.

The firefighter repeated new vital signs.

"Pulse is forty-five. Blood pressure eighty-five over fifty. How far away is that chopper?"

I took another deep breath and raised my head. Jorjana was strapped onto the gurney. One medic held the IV up high, and another monitored the blood pressure cuff—one guy at the foot of the gurney, another at the head.

They were efficient, these medics. And they were helping. Her face had regained some color, and her lips were pink. But efficient was one thing. I knew in my soul that she needed a friend.

I pushed my way past the efficient strangers and grabbed her hand.

"I'm here, Jorjana. Hang in there. We're trying to help you."

And then they took her away. I stayed as close as I could, trailing the gurney and its keepers, the firefighter with the radio, and the nurse. We passed the pool and went through the East Reception Hall and out the front doors. I took no notice of the other guests or whether they were ill or not. I did not see the other paramedics, the firefighters, or the cops. I barely noticed the line of York staff watching with tearful eyes or the line of fire trucks with flashing lights. I followed the gurney through the porte cochere and across the front lawn to the helipad, where a medical helicopter floated its way to the ground. I pushed my way up to Jorjana and once again took her hand.

"I'm here. Please, Jorjana, stay strong!"

The helicopter was noisy, and the downdraft from the blades sent loose bits of everything flying everywhere. But Jorjana heard me. In the midst of the noise and the wind and the chaos of fire trucks and medics and cops, she heard me.

She opened her eyes, turned her head ever so slightly, and looked right at me.

I knew exactly what she wanted to hear.

"I will take care of everything here. You get better, OK?"

She didn't nod exactly, but she lowered her chin just enough. And she gave my hand the gentlest of squeezes before closing her eyes.

Then the helicopter landed, and they took her away from me.

Watching that helicopter fly away was the hardest thing I had ever done.

Chapter Fifteen

The nurse guarding the entrance to the UCLA ICU didn't know what she was up against.

In the hours after the helicopter took Jorjana away, I directed the chaos at the York Estate. Stricken guests were carted away by ambulance. The police interviewed the well. Media helicopters circled above, which drove the army of German shepherds into a frenzy that just added to the noise. I called in a favor and got a helicopter to deliver one of Jorjana's private nurses to UCLA. I tracked Franklin down. As I headed to the hospital, the York plane was bringing him back from Alaska.

I'd done everything I'd promised Jorjana, and now I needed to see her.

"I'm here to see Jorjana York," I said.

"Are you family?"

"Yes."

"Your name?"

"Alana Fox."

The nurse was skeptical. She wasted time typing something into her computer. I spotted a list on her desk. I can read upside down, so I learned that Jorjana was in room 7. I walked right over to a pair of double doors and entered the ICU.

"Hey! You can't go in there!"

The nurse made the mistake of grabbing my arm. I spun around. I resisted decking her.

"I have Jorjana York's medical power of attorney. If you can't find my name, then call security. Meanwhile, let go of me. I'm going to my friend."

She let go.

I made it to room 7 without security showing up.

Jorjana looked awful. Her face was pale, her hair ratted about her head. There were tubes everywhere—a tube in her mouth, a multitude of IVs in her arm, and a catheter bag strapped to the side of the bed. The bag was empty. A small screen by the bed displayed wiggly lines in red and green—the data of her heartbeat, pulse, and temperature. There was a constant puffing of the oxygen machine. The room was dark. It did not sit well with me that she'd been alone.

I leaned over and gave her a kiss.

"It's me, Jorjana. Everything is fine at the house. Hang in there."

She didn't move. Not even a flinch. I've never felt so helpless in my life.

"Mrs. Fox?"

I turned around. Standing in the doorway was the private nurse. Behind her stood three men dressed in white lab coats. They all had stethoscopes around their necks. One of them held a clipboard. I'm no medical expert, but I figured they were Jorjana's doctors.

"Mrs. Fox? May we have a word?" This from one of the lab coats. As I left the room, Jorjana's private nurse slipped in. She gave me a quick hug and whispered, "She is in good hands. They have a plan."

The lab coats introduced themselves as the heads of ICU, nephrology, and gastroenterology. Between them there had to have been a hundred years of medical practice.

"I see you have Mrs. York's medical power of attorney?" Asked the guy with the clipboard, as he flipped through some papers.

I nodded.

"But Mrs. York is married?"

"Mr. York travels frequently," I explained. "Given Jorjana's..."

I didn't have to finish. They understood. Jorjana's health was fragile under the best of circumstances. Which saved me from explaining Franklin's fragile state of mind, which was the real reason that Jorjana had given me power of attorney for everything.

"Mrs. York ingested rhubarb leaves," said the GI doc.

I gasped. "Jorjana is allergic to rhubarb!"

"Yes, she is." The doc confirmed this by looking at his clipboard. "Mrs. York suffered an anaphylactic allergic reaction upon ingestion. Fortunately, the first responders got to her before she went into cardiac failure. We identified rhubarb in the vomit on her clothes and began treatment immediately. We are following the protocol to treat poisoning, but given that she is a paraplegic, we are concerned about her kidneys."

I had so many questions I didn't know what to say.

"The lab also found syrup of ipecac when they tested her vomit," the doc said, "which explains why so many people got sick so fast. We've informed the police and the other hospitals."

"The next few hours are critical." The nephrologist said. "Because of her allergy to rhubarb and her fragile health, there is the possibility of renal failure."

"Has her husband been notified?" The ICU guy.

I nodded and looked back into the room. Jorjana looked so frail, so lifeless.

The private nurse had kept me updated via text, but this was the first I had heard of rhubarb poisoning.

"Franklin is on his way," I said. "He should be here soon."

"Are there any other family members?" the ICU guy asked.

"No, just Franklin. And me." My voice was barely a whisper.

The doc consulted the clipboard. "And her niece."

"Niece?" I was confused.

The docs exchanged looks.

The ICU doc pointed to the private nurse sitting next to Jorjana.

"Her 'niece' arrived by helicopter shortly after Mrs. York. I assume more of Mrs. York's 'nieces' will come and go every eight hours or so?"

I was grateful they were willing to skirt ridiculous medical-privacy laws.

"Yes, Jorjana's nieces are very reliable that way," I said.

"We will continue to monitor her liver enzymes and watch her potassium levels. We are prepared to put her on dialysis if necessary. Right now we must wait and see how she responds."

They double-checked that they had my correct phone number and took their leave.

I joined Jorjana's "niece" by her side.

"She is in good hands, Mrs. Fox," the nurse said. "You should go home and get some sleep."

"No, I have to stay. Can we get another chair in there for me?"

"Why don't you go into the family waiting room?" She pointed down the hall. "I'll call you if Mrs. York needs you."

I hesitated.

"The best thing you can do is to take care of yourself. Mrs. York depends on you."

Guilt works wonders on me, even when I am not half out of my mind with worry. I decided to take the advice. I whispered to Jorjana that I would be just down the hall. Then I went down the hall.

The family waiting room was decorated in early despair, but thankfully, no one else was there. I sent a quick text message to David and Caroline before collapsing on a couch that smelled like sour milk. I lay there as wide-awake as if I had downed a triple espresso. Every time I closed my eyes, I saw Jorjana's pale face, her eyes closed, her breathing assisted by a machine. I was too tired to stay awake but too scared to close my eyes. I finally gave up.

I dug in my bag and pulled out my phone. Stan had just left a message. I looked up at a clock on the wall. It was 5:20 a.m. I wasn't the only one going without sleep.

He answered on the first ring. "How is Jorjana?" he asked.

I gave him the update.

"Rhubarb? How could rhubarb make so many people so sick?"

"There was syrup of ipecac in the salad dressing, too."

Stan said nothing, but I heard a click-click in the background. I wondered where he was. The last time I'd seen Stan, he had collected Maddie from under the kitchen table and was taking her home.

"Where are you?" I asked.

"I'm home. Maddie's asleep. I'm keeping in touch with the guys on the investigation."

The click-clicks continued. There was a pause and then, "Yeah, they knew about the rhubarb and the syrup of ipecac. That stuff is nasty. We kept it on hand when the kids were little, just in case."

"In case of what?"

"In case they ate something they shouldn't."

"Like rhubarb?"

"Yeah. Any idea who'd want to do this?"

I told him what Rusty had said about the threats to Ken. I heard more click-clicks before Stan answered.

"The guys will talk to Tuttle. He should have stuck around and answered questions with the rest of the folks."

Graham Tuttle's cavalry of black T-shirts couldn't have removed him from the York Estate faster if they had shot him off the property in a cannon. When I got back to the house after Jorjana was airlifted away, Graham Tuttle and Jack Jessup were already gone. No one knew how or when they had left—a fact that did not sit well with me.

"How are you doing?" Stan asked. I heard the typing continue in the background. It was probably killing him not to be in the middle of the investigation.

"I'm..."

I didn't get to answer. Stan stopped typing.

"Yeah, Maddie, I'm talking to Alana," he said. "OK, I'll be right there."

To me he said, "I gotta go, Alana. Maddie is scared."

I was scared too, dammit. Maddie wasn't the only one who needed Stan.

"When can we get together?" I managed to ask before he hung up.

"How about lunch?" Stan suggested. "Maddie and her mom have a therapy session at noon."

We agreed to lunch at Taverna Tony in the Malibu Country Mart. He hung up without saying "I love you." And that, too, did not sit well with me.

There was no way I was going to fall asleep now. I walked to a vending machine and decided against coffee. Things were bad enough already without resorting to vending machine coffee.

I eyed a TV hanging on the wall. I found the remote control and turned the thing on. And there in living color was Ken Wheeler on the early morning newscast.

"We are heartbroken that someone deliberately poisoned innocent people," Ken said. "This was a vicious attack..."

He acted gubernatorial; I gave him that. He was outraged in all the right places and promised justice in all the others. He commended the medics, the firefighters, the cops, and the hospital doctors and nurses. When asked questions by the reporters, he came across as if he, Ken Wheeler, were leading the investigation.

I was struck by how fresh he looked. I had last seen him around midnight, and he had looked pretty haggard. At some point Ken had changed clothes, brushed his hair, sharpened his dialogue, and got himself in front of cameras in time for the morning news shows. I gave him credit for his stamina. And I wondered what he added to his coffee.

Actually, I gave him credit for more than stamina. Ken had taken charge of a crisis and managed it masterfully. There was no telling what that hysterical crowd would have done if left to its own devices. Ken was a guy you could count on in an emergency—there was no doubt. And he and Lara had worked exceptionally well to see that all the families of the sick guests knew where their loved ones had been taken.

The TV cameras panned away as Ken finished making his statement. Lara and Spencer stood by his side. They, too, had freshened up. As the camera swung away from the Wheelers, I realized that Ken was making his statement on the front steps of the UCLA Medical Center, right around the corner from where I sat. I wondered what he was doing here.

With nothing better to do, I went to find out.

I found Ken, Lara, and Spencer in the hallway outside the ICU. Four guys dressed in black suits and wearing earphones hovered around them. They looked even more sinister than the black T-shirts that had guarded the dinner party. The suits wore mirrored sunglasses. I saw gun holsters under their jackets. I wondered if their sunglasses prevented them from seeing all the signs stating that the UCLA medical campus was a weapon-free site.

The Wheelers looked even fresher in person than on TV. I suspected that I looked as rumpled as I felt.

"What are you doing here?" I asked them. I didn't have the energy for niceties.

"We're visiting the guests who are in the hospital," Ken said. "It's the least I can do."

"How is Jorjana?" Lara asked.

"She went into anaphylactic shock and is in danger of renal failure. Did you know that someone put rhubarb leaves in the salad?"

They did not. Ken's face paled; Lara gasped and put her hand to her mouth. Spencer stiffened.

"Dad! You're allergic to rhubarb! They tried to kill you!" Spencer cried out. Ken put one arm around his son and the other around his wife.

"Who told you this?" Ken asked.

"Jorjana's doctors. She's allergic to rhubarb too."

Lara pulled away from Ken. She stepped away and began typing something fiercely on her phone. Ken spoke quietly to Spencer. The Wheeler family was having a moment. To my eyes, Lara was taking charge. I was willing to bet anything that her furious typing was going straight to Mac McDonald, and she wasn't thanking him for doing a good job of protecting her husband. When Lara stepped back, the three Wheelers stood shoulder to shoulder and presented a united front.

"Alana, this is disturbing," Lara said. "There have been threats to Ken's life. I'm certain that rhubarb was meant for him. It's fairly well known that he is allergic."

"What do you mean it's well known?"

Lara actually blushed. "My one and only effort to impress Ken with my culinary skills was to bake a strawberry rhubarb pie. Ken ended up in the hospital."

"There's a story about that on Dad's website," Spencer said gruffly. "It's kind of a family joke."

I thought of the black T-shirts at the gate and all the dogs that had been put into place to protect Ken Wheeler. And all someone had to do to hurt him was to visit his website.

Lara was thinking the same thing.

"I just alerted Mac," Lara said. "His security team should have prevented this."

No kidding. But then, who would have thought to hire a food taster?

Lara threw a glare at the four guys in suits standing behind them.

"As you can see, our security has been tightened. In hindsight."

The suits didn't flinch.

Lara turned her attention to her husband.

"Why don't you and Spencer visit the patients? I'd like to have a word with Alana."

Ken followed her orders and took off, with Spencer trotting behind. Two of the suits followed close on their heels.

Lara watched them go. Ken took a right turn at a hallway, while Spencer kept walking straight ahead, his head down, eyes on his phone. One of the suits followed Ken; the other one chased Spencer and turned him around.

"That may be a case of the blind leading the blind," Lara said with a sigh.

I didn't disagree.

"Have you had any sleep at all, Alana?"

"No."

"You look exhausted. But if I could just have a moment of your time?"

One mention of not sleeping, and I suddenly wanted nothing but to lie down. All I could think of was to check on Jorjana and then find a place to sleep. Specifically, in my very own bed in my very own home. So I needed to leave before the morning traffic made the drive into Malibu impossible. I told Lara as much.

"I will be brief. Let's have a seat over there."

I did not have the energy to argue. The two remaining suits and I followed her to a small alcove. Conveniently, there were two chairs. I sat facing Lara, and the suits stood with their backs to us, thus blocking my view of the ICU door.

"I am glad we ran into you, Alana," Lara said. "I intended to give you a call this morning."

I settled into the chair. Something told me I would have to hear her out.

"I was impressed by how you handled Ken last night before the dinner," Lara said. "Ken's enthusiasm can make it hard for him to focus. You knew just what to say to keep him on message."

"I was protecting Jorjana's interests," I said.

"I know, and that impressed me as well."

Lara leaned forward and looked me straight in the eye. It was a nice move. The alcove was tiny. I had to look right back at her or stare at the asses of the suits.

"Jorjana understands that the campaign is at a point where we need to tighten our message. To do that, we must have people on the team that Ken will listen to and that are not afraid to tell him things that he doesn't want to hear. You may recall that Jorjana offered her expertise to the campaign. Our intent is to help Ken focus on the important issues."

"Yes, I remember."

"We need to begin work immediately. I think you would be the perfect person to step into Jorjana's seat until she is well again."

"You want me to join the campaign?" I may have choked a bit right there.

"Not in an official capacity. As an advisor. Just until Jorjana recovers."

"Surely there is someone else…"

Lara wasn't done with her pitch. "This is very important to Jorjana."

Jorjana was a better person than me—she didn't need a reward to support a cause, the way I did. She supported causes because she felt it was the right thing to do. But now she couldn't follow through on something she had promised to do, and I knew that would bother her. As much as I hated to admit it, I'd promised Jorjana I'd take care of things for her. I had a duty to carry on when she couldn't.

Lara had me on the hook.

She reeled me in with an invitation. "Won't you come to dinner at Graham's tonight?"

And there it was—a reward for me.

Lest you think I could be bought, let me assure you that I could. Graham Tuttle's notorious privacy was eclipsed only by the notoriety that surrounded his home. Photos of the place were nonexistent, but I'd heard stories. About how the concrete foundation was vast enough to land a 747. About the miles of pipes and the acres of glass. About an organic vegetable farm, a herd of grass-fed cattle, and a well, dug down miles to siphon groundwater to support the vegetation. Someone knew someone whose cousin's best friend's sister was the interior decorator, and she said the furnishings were custom-made to fit Graham Tuttle's ass. I desperately wanted to see the place for myself.

I was in.

"What time should I be there?"

"We will have cocktails at six," Lara said. "Strategy will be discussed over dinner."

I took down the address to Graham Tuttle's home like I had no idea where it was. Just because I'd never been there didn't mean I didn't know where he lived.

As I stood to take my leave, Spencer walked up.

The suits parted and let the kid in.

Spencer looked like he had pulled an all-nighter. The bags under his eyes were big enough to sink a basketball. His skin had that pallor it gets on no sleep. He plopped onto the arm of his mother's chair and slumped against the wall.

"Spencer, where's Dad? Are you OK?"

"Dad sent me to find you. People are asking for you."

"Dad isn't by himself, is he?"

"Luke is with him. They're up on the fourth floor."

"Spencer, are you OK?" Lara asked again. She put her hand up to his forehead, that classic mother move that I never understood.

"I'm tired is all. Let's go find Dad." The kid stood up with effort.

Lara took him by the arm and turned him to face her.

"You are beyond tired, son. Go back and get some rest. Dad and I can take it from here."

"I'm staying with Dad," Spencer replied. His face had the stubborn look of a three-year-old gripping a forbidden lollipop.

Lara pulled him close for a hug and held on. "Dad will be safe. These guys won't let anyone near him. I promise."

Spencer closed his eyes and leaned into her shoulder. She whispered something into his ear. The suits shifted uncomfortably from one leg to another.

"Let's call an Uber for you, son," Lara said. She held Spencer out at arm's length. He took a deep breath, brushed a tear out of his eye, and nodded.

"I can take Spencer back to Malibu," I offered. "I'm heading back as soon as I check on Jorjana."

"If it's no trouble…" Lara's gaze shifted from Spencer to me to the suits.

"I'll be OK, Mom," Spencer said. "I promise to wait at the house for you and Dad."

Spencer gave his mother a hug.

"Fine, then. Thank you, Alana. I'll see you tonight."

I told Spencer I would be right back and went to see Jorjana.

Chapter Sixteen

Spencer immediately slumped into a chair and pulled out his phone. I knew enough about kids to know he would entertain himself. But a second look at him, and I wondered how long he would stay awake. The kid did look tuckered out.

Room 7 was crowded. Jorjana's nurse, a doctor, and Franklin York stood around her bed.

Franklin York is in his sixties. His hair is receding. His complexion is fair. He is tall and slender and gives an impression that he would be at content to live in a library and translate Scripture with a quill pen. Under the studious exterior lives a man who blames himself for the accident that killed his daughter and left his wife an invalid. When the pain of this guilt becomes too much for him, Franklin flees to go shoot things. He had been taking his guilt out on Alaskan elk when Jorjana was stricken. One look at him, and I knew he was again blaming himself for Jorjana's latest injury.

"How is she?" I whispered to no one in particular.

Jorjana looked pretty much the same to me. Pale, still, fragile.

"We are cautiously optimistic," the doctor said.

Franklin turned away from Jorjana and motioned for me to follow him. We ended up in the family waiting room with the milk-stained couch.

"How did this happen?" Franklin asked. His eyes were red. He was in need of a shower.

I gave him the condensed version of the events.

"I should have been with her," Franklin said.

"You couldn't have prevented this." I explained the security measures.

"They did not protect my wife," Franklin replied. His eyes welled up, and he collapsed onto the couch.

"No, they didn't." I had to agree that was true.

I have been a friend of Jorjana and Franklin's for nearly thirty years. I know them as well as if they were true kin. Jorjana gave me her medical power of attorney because she knew Franklin might crumble under emotional pressure if she fell ill. Now she was ill, and as I watched Franklin, I saw him start to crumble.

I summoned the last of my energy to pull him together. Fortunately, I knew how to rally him.

"Knock it off!" I scolded him like he was a truant little boy. "This was not your fault! The police are searching for whoever did this. Jorjana is in the best hands possible. You need to pick yourself up and let your wife know that you are here for her! Do not let her down, dammit!"

It worked. Franklin wiped his nose on the sleeve of his flannel shirt, took a deep breath, and stood up. From one of the pockets in his hunting vest, he pulled out a pill bottle. He got a cup of coffee from the vending machine and downed two pills with the awful stuff. Within moments, he was a new man.

"Thank you, Alana. I will be there for Jorjana."

I escorted him back to her room. The nurse looked up as we entered. I pointed to the clock on the wall, held up two fingers, and pointed to Franklin. She gave a discreet nod and made a note on a pad. I knew she would keep an eye on Franklin, too.

"I'm going home to get some sleep," I told Franklin and the nurse. "If anything happens, call me."

They promised they would. I gave Jorjana a kiss and left.

I was cautiously optimistic.

The UCLA Medical Center, being a world-class facility, has valet parking. Spencer and I made our way to the lobby, waited for the car to be fetched, and managed not to say a word to each other. Mostly because he hardly took his eyes from his phone.

He focused so hard on the screen and typed so furiously with his thumbs that I thought he would punch a hole in the screen. At least the kid was awake.

It wasn't until the car appeared that Spencer stopped beating up his phone.

"That's such a beautiful car, Mrs. Fox."

He snapped a photo of the car as the valet pulled it forward. Spencer looked more awake than I felt. So I offered to let him drive to Malibu.

"Really? Yeah, I'd love to!" He ran to the driver's side so fast the valet had to jump out of his way.

I gave the valet the tip and settled myself in on the passenger side. Spencer adjusted the seat and fastened his seat belt. He took another photo of the dashboard before putting the car in gear.

Vintage cars, no matter how well they are maintained, have nuances that can make them a bear to drive. I have a 1957 Fury that doesn't like to make right turns. The driver's-side door of my pink Porsche doesn't open. The Mustang has a sticky clutch. But Spencer proved to be a decent driver. He figured out how to manage the clutch in a nanosecond. Before I knew it, we were out of Westwood and heading north on PCH.

"Have you tried to fix the clutch?" Spencer asked.

"I keep forgetting to ask Fred to look into it."

"Fred's the guy who takes care of your cars, right? Where's your garage again?"

"It's out in Calabasas. Fred brings the cars in when I need them."

For a kid who had looked like he was about to fall into a sleep coma, Spencer sure was awake now. Awake and edgy, he cursed at a car that cut him off. I decided to distract him with the story of Fred.

"Fred delivered the mail to the house when I was married. That house had a fourteen-car garage. When Fred retired from the Postal Service, he asked if we needed anyone to maintain the cars. My ex-husband used to go through mechanics like crazy. When we divorced, I got the cars. And Fred."

"Guys like that are hard to come by."

"No kidding."

We drove on in silence. The fact that Spencer appreciated how valuable Fred was to me told me volumes about how much the kid knew about the vintage-car world. I remembered him mentioning that Ken had a Mustang at one time. I wondered where Ken would house a car. Most serious collectors stored their cars in warehouses that were climate controlled, security heavy, and kept as clean as a whistle. And then someone had to tend to the vehicles. Keeping a full-time mechanic on the payroll wasn't cheap, but it sure made life easier. Alan had been very particular about who took care of his cars. He used to run through mechanics like most people went through toilet paper.

My tired mind wandered away from the Mustang and on to those random thoughts that exhaustion brings on. I was running through a list of colors to paint the Mustang when Spencer stopped at the gates in front of the York Estate. I was surprised how quickly we'd gotten back to Malibu. And then I realized I had dozed off.

"This is where I get out. Thanks again, Mrs. Fox." Spencer put the car in park and hopped out.

"This is Jorjana's house," I said in foggy confusion.

"Yeah, we're staying with Mrs. York," Spencer said.

And then I remembered that David Currie had been called in to help the upstairs staff prepare for the Wheeler family's sleepover. Not that anyone got much sleep the previous night.

"Why don't I drive you up to the house?" I asked.

"I'll walk. I could use the exercise."

"Do you want me to get you through the gate at least?"

"Nah, they'll let me in. Thanks again, Mrs. Fox. Are you awake enough to drive home?"

I assured him that I was and bid him good-bye. As I drove away, he snapped another shot of the car.

And then I went home and collapsed into bed.

Chapter Seventeen

I got a whole four hours of sleep, took a criminally long shower, and dressed while downing a pot of coffee. Updates from the hospital told me that Jorjana was breathing on her own. The verdict on dialysis was still out. All of this was good enough news to keep me from returning to the hospital.

I had some time before my lunch date with Stan, so I put on another pot of coffee and went to the office at the back of my house. I checked emails and phone messages. Every message and e-mail concerned the disaster at the dinner. Everyone wanted to know everything. The sheer volume of it made my head ache.

I poured more coffee and attempted to tackle as much e-mail as I could. I started with Marjorie Dunham and reassured her that I would personally deliver her to the shopping outing of the Happy Hour Girls. Then I confirmed my presence for two cocktail parties and one restaurant soft opening. Then I started answering the e-mails regarding my well-being.

I ignored the calls coming in until the caller ID read "David Currie."

"David, how are you?"

"Frazzled, darling. How is Jorjana?"

I'd kept David and Caroline updated via texts throughout my hospital visit. It was a relief to actually talk to someone for a change.

"Franklin is there, and the latest report was that she is stable. The doctors are monitoring her kidney function."

"The prognosis?"

"If her kidneys hold up, I think the prognosis is good."

"Thank heavens for that. How are you, darling?"

"Exhausted. Worried."

I paused as I remembered Jorjana's white face and all the tubes running in and out of her.

"And angry. Have you heard anything new?"

"No, darling, but I do think your opinion of Ken was a bit harsh. Ken was very impressive last night."

"Yeah, Ken handled the crowd really well."

"Perhaps you were wrong in labeling the man a nitwit, darling. He does handle a crisis calmly. Which he may need when it comes to his own family. I heard some interesting tidbits about the Wheeler clan."

I really didn't care, but David was incapable of sitting on a good bit of gossip. I told him to spill.

"Well, it seems that oldest boy did not leave school willingly. Apparently, young Spencer was spending more time betting at the track than in the library at UoP. Word is that he ran into a string of bad luck and owed a *loan shark* a bundle. A *loan shark*! Can you just imagine the look on Lara Wheeler's face when she heard that, darling?"

I remembered the look on her face when Graham Tuttle had said something about Spencer being a good kid. I wondered if Graham knew about Spencer's gambling debts.

"So, I heard that Ken bailed the boy out of the mess and then ordered him to work on the campaign."

"Interesting for sure," I said as I shut down my computer. "It's certainly easy to lose money on those stupid racehorses. But does this have anything to do with figuring out who poisoned Jorjana? Ken and Lara think the rhubarb was intended to harm him. Apparently he is allergic, too."

"No, darling, young Spencer's troubles have nothing to do with our Jorjana."

"Ask around, will you? Rusty said there were threats made against Ken, and obviously, someone made good on them. Someone knows something."

"Will do, darling. Keep me posted on Jorjana."

We said our good-byes, and then it was time for my lunch with Stan.

Taverna Tony is a Greek restaurant that has been around long enough that no one can remember when it opened. The outdoor patio is charming, the indoors reminiscent of a Spanish villa. I prefer the place at lunchtime because the likelihood of encountering belly dancers is greatly diminished. The hostess greeted me by name and said I was the first of my party to arrive.

I was already fifteen minutes late.

She led me to my favorite table, up in the loft, overlooking the whole place. She took my order for an iced tea and left me alone to wait for Stan. I was on my second iced tea by the time he showed up.

Stan arrived wearing my favorite outfit—jeans with a white button-down shirt and sandals. He looked exhausted. I suspected he'd had as much sleep as I had. His face was puffy, and he carried himself like it was an effort to draw a breath. I probably should have felt sympathy for him.

But he didn't arrive alone. Maddie was with him.

Maddie had circles under her eyes and gripped her father's hand like he was the only tether keeping her on earth. She wore her school uniform, but her skirt was not rolled up to her butt. She carried a backpack. She looked relieved to see me.

"I'm sorry I'm late, but we had an issue this morning," Stan said. His eyes begged me to understand.

"What happened?" I only asked because I knew it was expected. If I were interested in threesomes, I would have dated a different kind of guy.

"Maddie is afraid to go to school." Stan pulled a chair out for her. She chose to sit next to me.

"I saw a UFO last night," Maddie said, with her eyes as big as flying saucers. "It was, like, flying around the pool when all the people were, like, gagging."

"Maddie, sweetie, we've gone over this and..."

"Wait a minute." I put my hand up to stop Stan. And then I said to Maddie, "What did it look like?"

"It was about this big." She put her hands up to show me. A shoebox would have fit in the space. "And it was black, and it had, like, legs and stuff, and it went like this." Maddie blew through her lips and did a spot-on imitation of a drone.

I turned to Stan. "It was a drone. There was one flying outside Jorjana's suite before the dinner. Whoever flew it might have photos your guys can use."

Stan was on it. "Order something for me. I'll be right back." And he left with his phone to his ear.

I turned to Maddie and said, "Now, let's you and I discuss which one of us is going to date your father."

I wouldn't say the lunch went swimmingly, but it wasn't a disaster, either. The three of us settled on the topic of Jorjana.

I told the story of how Jorjana and I had met. "So there I was, new to Malibu, and Jorjana shows up on my front doorstep with a pitcher of margaritas and a platter of cookies..."

Stan did the color commentary on the decor of the York Dining Room. "There must be a hundred stuffed heads on those walls..."

Maddie managed to show some maturity and worried about Jorjana. "Is Mrs. York going to be OK?"

That did bring the conversation to a halt. Neither Stan nor I could hide our concern. Maddie excused herself to go to the restroom.

I wasted no time. "She should be in school, Stan."

"She was upset. I couldn't send her to school like that."

"She is always upset," I said. "And no wonder. Being upset gets her out of everything she doesn't want to do."

"You sound like you don't like her."

"It doesn't matter if I like her or not. She needs to go to school every day, whether she is upset or not."

"She really needed me today, Alana."

"So did I."

This was getting us nowhere. I needed him. His kids needed him. And he did his damnedest to be in two places at once. I got it. I didn't like it, but I got it.

Stan took my hand and smiled that smile of his. Damn him.

"Let me make it up to you. Maddie is staying with my sister tonight, and I don't have to be on duty until midnight. Let's go to Gravina for dinner."

It was a sweet gesture. Gravina is my favorite Italian restaurant. By Malibu standards, it is reasonably priced. But Stan was supporting an ex-wife and four kids on a cop's salary. Gravina would shoot a hole in his budget. The fact he was willing to take the hit spoke volumes. Unfortunately, I had other plans.

"I can't. Something has come up unexpectedly."

As soon as I said it, I knew how it sounded.

"It's OK for you to have unexpected things come up?" The look on Stan's face made my heart ache.

I'd like to say we worked it through, but after lunch we parted without so much as a hug. I don't know what was worse, that or the frightened look on Maddie's face.

Chapter Eighteen

I figured a walk couldn't possibly hurt me. I walked around the outer perimeter of the Country Mart. I passed the Malibu Town Center, where my office was located. I crossed the street at the library. I kept going up Civic Center Way, skirting the edge of the road and ignoring the stares of Malibu motorists unused to seeing pedestrians in any shape or form. I turned right at the three-way stop and headed up the hill to the Malibu Racquet Club. I sat on a bench outside the courts and listened to the thwack of tennis balls. I knew how those balls felt—constantly being shot from one place to the next, with no power to make it stop.

I don't like not being in control. I like plans and spreadsheets and schedules. I like waking up in the morning and knowing those damn waves outside my house will wash in and out all day long, no matter what. I like engraved invitations that arrive in the mail with enough time to ponder the RSVP. I like manners and traditions and the seasons predictably following each other. I do not like last-minute changes, cell phones ringing in restaurants, and broken promises.

It's not that I don't know how to handle unpredictable situations or people. It's just that I don't like to. And I am at a point in my life that I shouldn't have to put up with that nonsense if I don't want to.

And yet I was in a relationship with a guy with four kids and a vicious ex-wife. It didn't get much more unpredictable than that.

Unless you tossed in advising a guy who was running for governor.

Somehow, in less than twenty-four hours, a teenager and a politician—two sources of drama that I normally avoided like e-mail invitations—had upended my well-ordered life.

I left the tennis courts and walked back to my office. I allowed myself to wallow in self-pity all the way back. Then I let myself into the office, picked the mail up off the floor, and set about restoring order to my life. I began by remembering my priorities.

First, I called Jorjana's nurse for an update. The nurse answered on the first ring.

"Hello, Mrs. Fox. Mrs. York is awake. She can't talk just yet, but I will put the phone up to her ear so you can talk to her."

I heard the nurse tell Jorjana who was on the phone and then muffled instructions to "go ahead."

"It's me. I know you are in good hands, but I am worried sick about you."

More muffled noises, and then the nurse telling Jorjana not to talk. I tried to think what Jorjana would want to know before continuing.

"Caroline has everything under control at the house. The staff is fine, and you are not to worry about anything except getting better."

I had no idea if the staff was fine or not, but I knew Jorjana would worry about everyone but herself. Which brought me to my next bit of news for her.

"Lara Wheeler invited me to dinner at Graham Tuttle's tonight in your place. I will take lots of notes and get back to you. I know Franklin is with you, so you won't see me until tomorrow. Get some rest. I love you."

The nurse came back on the phone.

"Mrs. York is doing much better. But her blood pressure is still elevated, and the doctors are monitoring her lungs. She most likely will not need dialysis after all. She'll be here at least another two days."

"Does she know what happened?"

"Yes, the FBI was here. She is pretty distressed about it. I think she will feel better once they know who did this."

"Won't we all?"

I told the nurse to keep me posted and rang off.

I took a few minutes to remind myself that Jorjana was in the best hospital and under the best care. I could not make matters better if I were there, so the best thing I could do was to watch over Jorjana's interests in Malibu. Like it or not, her interests revolved around Ken Wheeler's campaign for governor. So I would go to the dinner at Graham Tuttle's house, take copious notes, and advise Ken to the best of my ability. I would do it for Jorjana. And I would get to see the inside of Graham Tuttle's house. So it wasn't all awful.

That settled, I turned my attention to my own business. I purposely avoided making phone calls. Based on the e-mails, all anyone still wanted to know about was the dinner. I decided to leave replying for later, when I could throw in tidbits about dining with Graham Tuttle.

I shut down my computer, gathered my bag, and locked the office. I had plenty of time for a long bath and a stiff drink. Both of which I needed desperately.

As I descended the stairs to the parking lot, I pondered what to wear to dinner. Good shoes, to start. Probably something black and minimalist. Nothing that said I was trying too hard. I mentally inventoried my closet as I wandered through the parking lot in search of my car. I had a nice silk tunic that took me to a lot of shindigs, but I decided it was too cocktail-ish. I could go with the black jersey wrap dress and gold accessories, but that also behaved best at a cocktail party. Since this was more of a business dinner, I thought of a nicely tailored pair of pants and a lightweight cardigan with a silk camisole underneath. I could get away with some artsy accessories with that outfit. I weighed the advantages of gold versus silver necklaces. Silver won.

Outfit planned, I stopped. I had made two laps around the parking lot. Where was my car? I turned around. My car was nowhere to be seen. I racked my tired brain to remember which car I was actually looking for. The downside of owning twelve cars was that I often forgot which one I was driving.

I thought hard. I'd parked the car in the lot and walked over to Taverna Tony to meet Stan for lunch. And it was the Mustang. I remembered because I'd let Spencer drive it back from the hospital. So where was it?

I took another tour up and down the lot. There were two Bentleys, three Teslas, and eight Range Rovers (black, of course). A variety of lesser BMWs and Mercedeses. Not one single sinus-infection-yellow 1966 Mustang to be found.

I stood in the middle of the lot and dialed 911.

Chapter Nineteen

It turns out a stolen car isn't a 911 problem. Once the operator established that no gun was involved, and no one had been abducted, I was transferred to another line, where I was promptly put on hold.

I used this time to find someone who actually cared about me. I knew exactly where to find him.

I let myself into the workroom at Errands, Etc. Three giant whiteboards on one wall were filled with David Currie's neat printing. Most of the day's errands were checked off. Two of David's staff were busying themselves putting together gift baskets—a favorite around Malibu and a big income producer for Errands. One of the ladies pointed down the hall to David's office.

David was on the phone when I entered. He held up one finger. I showed him my phone and made a face. I took a seat in a comfy chair and waited.

"Yes, darling, we will have the baskets delivered on time. The girls are putting them together as we speak. Yes, I know it is important. Yes, I have the address. I know you do. Yes, I know the address. Yes, darling. OK. Good-bye now."

David hung up his phone and pretended to collapse on his desk. I chuckled in spite of myself. David Currie could make the Grinch feel like the little bluebird of happiness.

"I'm on hold," I said, holding up my phone. "My car was stolen."

"No! Darling, when?"

"Well, if I knew that...oh, wait, someone is on the line now."

I spent the next ten minutes convincing the guy on the other end that I was absolutely positive that I had not parked in a tow zone, that I absolutely knew that no one else in my family had driven it away, and that I was absolutely certain that I had parked it where I said I had. I did stress that it was a vintage Mustang and not some fly-by-night Toyota. The guy responded that he figured it wasn't a Toyota since I was calling from Malibu. His sarcasm did not encourage me.

I gave him the license number, make, and model. I told him I would have to get back to him with the vehicle identification number. The call ended with his assurance that the cops would look out for it. I had my doubts.

"Good Lord, darling, what else could possibly go wrong today?"

David Currie was the most decent man I knew. If he weren't gay, I would insist on marrying him. He presented himself as Malibu's Gadfly About Town, but he was as even-keeled, smart, and loyal as they come.

"Thanks again for helping out last night," I said. "I don't know what I would have done without you. How was everything when you left?"

"Running smoothly, darling. The night staff came back onto the property since the Wheelers didn't stay after all, and by the time the cops left, you would hardly have known there had been an incident."

"What do you mean the Wheelers didn't stay?"

"They didn't stay overnight. That awful Mac person insisted it wasn't safe and moved them over to the Swanson place on Broad Beach Road. Good heavens, darling, what's the matter?"

I told him about running into the Wheelers at the hospital and bringing Spencer back to Malibu with me. "He got out at the drive leading up to the York Estate. He said he would walk up because he needed the exercise."

"Well, that is curious. Maybe he left something he needed to pick up. It was rather chaotic, if you remember. How is Jorjana?"

I gave him the update and then told him about my lunch with Stan.

"Oh, my poor darling. What you need is a drink. What say you and I just pop over to Nobu and have a little something?"

"I can't. I have this thing tonight."

I brought him further up to speed on Lara Wheeler's invitation to dinner.

"*Well!* Dinner at Graham Tuttle's...well, that is something!"

For David, that was almost speechless.

It was then I remembered that I had no way of getting to Graham Tuttle's house.

"Can you drive me up there? I can get the Wheelers to bring me home."

Could he? He could indeed.

"What will you wear, darling? Never mind, I will pick something out. But you look just exhausted! We need to get you into a hot bath with a nice cool drink, and I will find something suitable. I'm thinking black. What are the odds of bringing me along as your plus one, darling?"

David did more than find something suitable for me to wear. He ran the tub and mixed up The Usual. While I soaked and sipped, he tut-tutted his way through my closet.

"When was the last time you went shopping, darling? I haven't seen some of these styles since the first Bush was in office."

"I can still get into those clothes!"

"That doesn't mean you should. Oh, wait. This might work."

I came out of the tub to find that he had assembled the black pants, ivory silk camisole, and knobby knit cardigan that I'd had in mind. But none of my accessories would do. Not a one.

"Darling, you are dining with a billionaire. You must look the part. Why you didn't stock up on diamonds while you were married I'll never understand. Not to worry, I have an idea. But first, into bed with you. There is time for a nap, and goodness knows you look like you could use some beauty sleep!"

I didn't argue. I fell into bed while he zipped over to the Malibu Colony Company to pick up "the perfect little necklace I saw there yesterday." I was asleep before I thought to ask how much "the perfect little necklace" was going to cost me.

It was a good thing, too. That price tag would have kept me awake for a month.

"You look just lovely, darling! Spin around. Let me see you from behind."

I spun. I had to admit I felt pretty lovely. The bath, the nap, and another cocktail while I dressed did wonders for me. David's perfect little necklace was, well, perfect. A confection of mixed metals and freshwater pearls, it was sophisticated and unique. It pulled the whole outfit together without making me look like I was trying too hard.

To make things even better, the latest report was that Jorjana was out of the woods. I couldn't have felt better if I'd had a full night's sleep.

I gave David a kiss. "Thank you. I love it."

"You are welcome, darling. Now we must be on our way. You can't keep Graham Tuttle waiting."

"I'm ready, and thanks again for driving me. I could have asked Fred but...oh!"

"What is it, darling?"

"I forgot to ask Fred what the VIN is on the Mustang. I was supposed to give it to the guy who took the report."

"No worries, darling. You can call Fred on the way there. I doubt the police are putting all their men on this case."

"No kidding. I'll be lucky to ever see that car again. I guess I need to contact the insurance agent, too."

"Call on the way, darling. We have to go!"

Chapter Twenty

FRED (THE CALABASAS GARAGE)

"Some of the guys are hanging out at the Ventura Bar and Grill," Wes said. "A burger and a cold one sound good to me tonight. You want to come along?"

Fred finished washing the last cup and turned it upside down in the dish rack. He pulled the plug to the sink and wiped down the counter as the water drained away. He liked to keep things neat and tidy in his apartment.

"I think I'm gonna stay in tonight, Wes. Say 'hey' to the guys for me."

"You sure? Eddie's got a theory on the car thefts."

Fred laughed. "Eddie's got a theory on everything."

"I think he is on to something. He was just..."

Wes was interrupted. The tune "The Bitch Is Back" rang on Fred's phone.

"Just a second, Wes. That's Alana calling," Fred said. On the phone, he said, "Hi, Alana. Are you ready for me to bring down a new car?"

Fred's demeanor went from calm to furious in seconds.

"When did this happen?" he asked.

The tone of Fred's voice sent a shock through Wes. He knew that tone, and he didn't want to be in the same room with it.

"Why didn't you call me right away? There's a GPS on the Mustang."

Alana's answer did not please Fred. He listened for a moment longer before turning to his desk and picking up a pen.

"Give me the guy's number. I'll call with the VIN and tell him about the GPS. Got it. Right. Fine. Bye."

Fred hung up and closed his eyes. Wes had seen this before, and he knew Fred was struggling to apply anger-management techniques. Wes cowered on the couch in case the techniques failed, and Fred needed to hurt something. Wes wondered if he could hide under the coffee table if need be.

"Someone stole the Mustang this afternoon," Fred said when he opened his eyes. "Alana just now got around to telling me about it."

"That's awful, Fred," Wes said as neutrally as he could.

"She didn't sound too upset by it," Fred said. "Why the hell did she wait so long to call me?"

"You must be really upset," Wes said.

What had the counselor said? Don't contradict, just validate? Like Fred was some kind of parking ticket or something.

Wes didn't hold much stock in psychology. He had gone with Fred to see the counselor all those years ago because Fred needed a friend to help him out. But it had been a long while since Fred needed "handling." Fred kept himself in line with a disciplined schedule and caring for the cars and staying off the booze. But now something had happened to one of the cars. Wes sat stock-still and tried to remember how to handle one of Fred's blow-ups.

"I gotta call the cops with the VIN," Fred said. "Give me a second, OK?"

"OK." Neutral. Keep still.

Fred punched the number into his phone so hard that Wes was surprised the screen didn't split.

"This is Fred Winthrop calling. I have the VIN on the '66 Mustang that Alana Fox reported stolen." Fred recited the VIN from memory. "There's a GPS on it. You want the tracking number?"

The answer did not please Fred. He closed his eyes again. Wes eyed the floor under the coffee table.

"Yeah, that's too bad, but don't you have a separate division for stolen vehicles? Sure. Right."

Fred hung up and threw the phone on his desk.

"There's a fifteen-car pileup on the 101 in Camarillo, and every cop from Santa Barbara to San Diego is busy."

Fred sat at his desk and turned on his computer.

"You must be really upset," Wes said again. It seemed to work earlier. Fred hadn't thrown anything. Yet.

"Damn cops are useless," Fred muttered as the screen lit up.

He typed something on the keyboard. The screen showed a map with a blinking red light in one corner.

"The Mustang is in Camarillo. I'll have to go get it myself."

"I'll go with ya." Wes felt it best not to let Fred out in public alone.

Fred picked up his phone and typed in something. After a moment he compared the screen on his phone to the computer.

"OK, I've got it tracking on my phone. Let's go. We'll take the truck."

Fred stood up and grabbed a set of keys from a key rack. Then he reached into the pocket of a jacket hanging by the door. His hand came out with a gun.

"Fred, you're not supposed to have a gun!" Wes cried out.

Fred checked the safety and then handed the gun to Wes.

"If anyone asks, it's yours."

Wes kept an eye on the GPS on the phone as Fred drove the 1954 Chevy truck to Camarillo. To avoid the pileup on the 101, Fred took back roads through the Santa Monica Mountains before dropping down to PCH in north Malibu. The detour added more time to the trip than Fred would have liked, but the tracking device never moved.

"I wonder where they have it stashed," Wes said. "This map makes it look like it is out in a field."

"Somebody's barn probably," Fred said. "When I get my hands on whoever…"

"Maybe we should just call the cops," Wes suggested as neutrally as possible.

"Yeah, they've been so much help already."

PCH veered inland once they reached the Ventura County line. Wes read the directions as Fred took a turn onto Pleasant Valley Road. The area was agricultural, with endless stretches of strawberry fields on either side of the road. Wes told Fred to turn right at a dirt road.

"Are you sure?" Fred brought the truck to a stop. They both looked around. Miles and miles of strawberries surrounded them.

"Where would they stash the car?" Wes asked. "I don't see a barn or anything around here."

"Tell me when we get right opposite that flashing light."

Fred put the truck in gear and drove slowly down the road. About five hundred feet later, Wes told him to stop. The two men clambered out of the truck and stood staring at the field. Wes felt it best to leave the gun in the truck.

"Do you think they buried it?" Wes asked.

Fred grunted. He stepped off the road and into the strawberries.

Wes followed, his eyes on the screen. He was so engrossed in watching the flashing red light that he didn't see Fred stop. Wes walked right into him.

"What's the matter, Fred?"

Fred stood so still that Wes thought the man had stopped breathing. Fred was staring straight ahead at something on the ground. Wes followed his gaze and then gasped.

A man lay face down on the ground. In his hand was the GPS device. Blood stained his shirt the color of the strawberries on the plants around him.

Wes's head spun. His knees felt weak. Before he hit the ground, he could have sworn he heard Fred say, "Oh no, Wheeler. What have you done now?"

Chapter Twenty-One

Graham Tuttle's house was located up Latigo Canyon, about halfway between the Pacific Ocean and the moon. The road was narrow enough that David had to focus on maneuvering his cumbersome Errands, Etc. truck through the twists and turns. I kept myself busy notifying everyone who needed to know about my missing Mustang. I was just irritated enough about lunch that I decided Stan did not need to know. The conversations I had with Fred and the insurance agent did not put me in any more of a party mood.

"This is going to take forever to straighten out," I said to David. "Why did they steal my car?"

"It is a shame, darling, but maybe now you can buy a new car?"

"I still have eleven cars. Why do I need another one?"

Just then David's cell phone rang.

"So you can do this," David said. He pushed a button on the steering wheel.

"Sandy, darling! Guess where I am going?"

A woman's voice sang through the truck cab.

"I was calling to see if you wanted to go to dinner, David. Don't tell me you have a better offer!"

"Say hello to Alana, darling. I don't have a better offer—she does! I am delivering her to a dinner at Graham Tuttle's homestead. Tell me you are impressed!"

"Hi, Alana! I am impressed! Why is David driving you? Don't you have a hundred cars?"

"Just twelve," I said. "Or eleven. One of them was stolen today, which is why I need a ride."

David butted in then and went into great detail about the car being stolen right out from under my nose, helping me dress for dinner, and why I was invited to Graham Tuttle's in the first place. He didn't make stuff up, but he did embellish a bit on the details.

"Sounds marvelous," Sandy said. "I want to know everything tomorrow. Maybe you can talk to Ken Wheeler about your car, Alana. I knew Ken and Lara when I lived in San Francisco. He had a car stolen once. If I remember correctly, it was a Mustang."

"He mentioned that he had a Mustang," I said. "But he didn't say anything about it being stolen."

"It was about ten years ago. I was still married to the a-hole," Sandy said. "Ken bought this vintage Mustang from some guy in San Jose. He should have known better. I mean San Jose is hardly Pacific Heights. It turned out the car was stolen. Ken figured this out somehow and alerted the cops. He helped them catch the guy, and it broke up a whole ring of car thieves. Ken went to court to testify and everything. It was quite the big deal."

"Maybe he has some tips on how to handle the insurance claim," I said.

"I'll just bet he does. Take lots of notes and call me tomorrow!"

"David Currie delivering Alana Fox." David spoke out his window to a keypad mounted near a wooden gate. He used his formal tone of voice, which always surprised me when I heard it.

Graham Tuttle's gate was nowhere as elaborate as the gate that guarded the York Estate, but it was no less intimidating. It stood at least two stories high and looked solid enough to deter missile-bearing tanks. There were cameras mounted in plain sight on each side of the gate. They looked like they meant business. The metal fence that cordoned off Graham Tuttle's property bore signs proclaiming the fence was electric. The entire setup was not exactly a welcome mat.

Two cameras swiveled from side to side and then up and down. David pointed to the rearview mirror. I turned around and saw two more cameras mounted in trees across the street. They, too, gave the van a good once-over. I wondered where Graham Tuttle stashed the dogs and the Bunyans in T-shirts.

"Smile, darling, you're being videotaped!" David chuckled as the gate swung open. We were in.

A long drive led us to even higher elevations, through more gates that opened magically as we approached and past more cameras mounted in trees. The road eventually took a turn around a grove of date palms, and at long last, I laid eyes on Graham Tuttle's house.

None of the stories had prepared me to see the place in person.

Graham Tuttle's house looked like someone had cut a slit in the side of the mountain and inserted a glass wall. A driveway wound under a cover that jutted out from the glass. Native grasses were planted below the glass—no doubt required by the planning commission, which managed to look the other way when Graham Tuttle dug a hole in the mountain.

At the front entrance, an enormous steel door stood wide open. Just inside the door stood a butler holding a tray with a glass of wine. Apparently I was expected.

David pulled up under the cover. As the van came to a stop, two men appeared out of nowhere. I recognized them as two of the black suits that had guarded the Wheelers at the hospital. David rolled down his window and kept his hands on the wheel.

"Good evening, Mrs. Fox." One of the suits opened my door.

"Will you be waiting for Mrs. Fox this evening, Mr. Currie?"

The second suit was on David's side of the car, and his tone of voice suggested it was in David's best interest to not stick around.

"Mrs. Fox was hoping the Wheelers could drive her home," David said.

"Of course. Good evening then, Mr. Currie."

"Please come with me, Mrs. Fox." The other suit offered his hand to me.

I hesitated. Oddly, despite all the security, I felt very unsafe. I looked at David.

"It's all right, darling. Do it for Jorjana."

Well, for Jorjana then.

I stepped out of the truck and made a beeline for the glass of wine.

The suits accompanied my glass of wine and me through the house. Just inside the steel door was a circular reception area topped off with a glass roof. The floors were zebrawood and the walls bamboo. Not bamboo wood—real bamboo planted in the ground. Metal sculptures played hide-and-seek in the thick brush.

The house was, indeed, carved into the side of the mountain. One long expanse of glass faced south and provided the kinds of views you usually only got from a helicopter. The ceiling was exposed rock. The floors were concrete. We walked through a room that sported a bar built from the rock and a lounge area oriented to the view. We passed a dining area that was set for dinner. I saw that we would be a party of fourteen. A grand staircase carved into the rock led to an upper floor.

We ran out of house at a pair of zebrawood doors. One of the suits opened it and indicated that I was to enter. As I stepped into the room, I heard the door close with a solid thunk behind me.

I expected a living room cut from the rock like the rest of the house. I expected custom-made furnishings perfectly aligned to the shape of Graham Tuttle's ass. I expected servers passing tiny hors d'oeuvres. I really wanted another glass of wine. What I found was something else altogether.

The room was a glass dome, and it seemed to float over the canyon below. Telescopes lined the glass walls—huge telescopes with lenses the size of truck tires. The furnishings—low couches—crowded the middle of the room. This was not a room for socializing. This was a room for an astronomer. An astronomer with a few billion extra bucks to throw around.

The astronomer—Graham Tuttle himself—was peering into one of the telescopes and speaking in an excited voice. Around him stood Ken and Lara Wheeler and a few other folks, all trying their damnedest to look interested. It appeared that I was not the only one in the room dying for another drink.

"If you look right here, you will see Venus. As soon as the sun sets, I can show you the constellation Caelum, which is my personal favorite. I had this room built specifically to capture Caelum's beauty, and I know you will agree once you see it."

Ken handed his drink to Lara and obligingly peered into the scope. Just then Lara spotted me. She seemed particularly glad of it.

"Oh, Graham! Alana is here!"

Lara pulled Graham Tuttle away from his stargazing. He looked about as happy to see me as a dog would be to see the vet.

"How is Jorjana?" Graham asked.

"She is expected to make a full recovery."

"Good. Come meet the others."

The "others" were more than happy to step away from the telescopes and greet me. There were ten of them, and I either knew or had heard of them all. The owner of the TV station that provided the helicopter ride for Jorjana's nurse took my hand and introduced me around. It was an eclectic group assembled from around the state. The group included an assemblyman from Stockton, two Silicon Valley gazillionaires, the guy who controlled all the agriculture concerns in the Central Valley, the guy who owned the telecommunications operations in San Diego, the guy who ran the wine industry in Napa Valley, the guy who ran the movie studio that dictated what teenagers saw every summer, a lawyer—and Alan Fox.

I nodded to Alan and focused on the other guys.

All guys. Every last one of the advisors was a man, and a couple of them were well-known supporters of the opposing party. I wondered if Lara had invited Jorjana to join just so she would have another female opinion. And then I wondered why the guys from the other party were there.

I reported on Jorjana's health to each guy. I knew what was going on—I was being vetted by each and every one of them, even the ones who knew me—which annoyed me, since I suspected each and every one of them had received an updated dossier on me before I arrived.

I talked to Alan last.

My ex-husband and I faced off near one of the telescopes. He is not a bad- looking guy, Alan. He is a few years older than me, which would put him in his mid-fifties by the time his next batch of kids arrived. His hair is graying. The green eyes that had captivated me at eighteen now hid behind thick glasses. He is not a genius, but he isn't stupid either. He is a nice man, which is his greatest fault. Alan Fox spends entirely too much time making certain everyone is happy.

"Are you OK, Alana? How is Jorjana, really?" Alan started right in worrying about everyone else.

"I'm OK. I'm tired, but I'm less worried." I gave him the latest on Jorjana.

"She's going to be OK. That's good, that's good. Tori and I were really concerned."

I stiffened as I automatically do whenever LMTB's name was mentioned. But then I remembered how helpful Tori had been in tending to the stricken guests. She'd worked side by side with the paramedics to evaluate the sick and comfort the frightened. She and Alan only left the York Estate after the last guest went home.

"Tori was a lot of help last night," I said without so much as choking on one word. I got points for that.

Alan visibly relaxed. And then went straight to an unrealistic expectation.

"She's a good girl, Alana. You would like her if you gave her a chance."

"I said I appreciated her help, Alan. I didn't say I wanted to be friends."

Alan looked properly chastised. You would think the man would have learned by now. I changed the subject.

"What are you doing here, Alan?"

"Graham asked me to be an advisor for Ken's campaign. I wasn't going to come. I didn't want to leave Tori and the kids alone after last night, but she thought it was a good idea, so here I am."

"How do you know Graham?"

Alan hesitated in that annoying way he has. He managed to answer before I shook the words out of him.

"I don't really *know* him. Jack Jessup contacted me a couple of weeks ago about some property we have for sale in Stockton and said Graham was interested. So I met with Graham, and then he thought Ken and I would hit it off. Tori and I had them over for dinner."

That explained why I didn't know Alan and Graham had met. It happened after the last board meeting. And the story about the dinner matched Ken's version. At least that little mystery was cleared up.

"What kind of advice does Graham want from you?" I asked.

Alan wasn't the only one under interrogation. On the other side of the room, each advisor took a turn at Ken Wheeler. And it didn't appear to go well. As I questioned Alan, Ken Wheeler spent a lot of time arguing a point as his advisors frowned.

Meanwhile, Lara planted herself on a couch and made phone calls. By the look on her face, she wasn't extending well wishes to supporters. Ken glanced over her from time to time. Each time she met his gaze with a shake of her head. Then she returned to her phone. Like mother, like son. I remembered Spencer's fascination with his phone at the hospital. Had it only been that morning?

The cocktail hour dragged on so long that the sun set over the Santa Monica Mountains. The stars came out, and Graham Tuttle all but skipped over to the telescope.

"We can see Caelum now!"

The rest of us did not share his enthusiasm.

Jack Jessup, Graham's attorney, saved me from the stargazing.

"Mrs. Fox, will you follow me?"

It wasn't a question.

I left Alan and followed Jack Jessup out of the dome room and into the hallway of the main house. We ascended the staircase carved out of the rock. At the top of the stairs, another hallway ran the length of the house. A rock wall ran down one side, and a series of zebrawood doors ran down the other. Jessup opened a door and ushered me in.

We entered a room that could only be Graham Tuttle's office. Three of the walls were bookshelves. The fourth was glass. The view was pretty much what you would expect. A glass desk was set at an angle to enjoy the view. In the very far distance, lights from Malibu shimmered. A couple of couches took up the rest of the room. Jack indicated that I was to sit.

I sat. And I can tell you the rumor that the furniture was built to accommodate Graham Tuttle's ass was way off. That stuff wasn't built to accommodate the ass of any human being. The couch was one of those artsy contraptions that looked interesting but were impossible to get comfortable in. I perched as best I could on the edge. Jessup did not waste any time concerning himself with my comfort.

"I don't trust you," he began. "But Lara seems to think you or Jorjana can get Ken to listen."

Of all the surprises I'd had that day, this was not one of them. Jessup had looked at me like a vegetarian views roast beef all evening.

"Are you staying?" he asked.

"You mean for dinner?"

"No, for the floor show."

His sarcasm irritated me. I kept my mouth shut.

"Of course, for dinner," he continued. "Because if you are, you need to know that anything you hear at the table does not leave the room. Do you understand?"

I do not intimidate easily. I met his bravado and raised it.

"I'm here to represent Jorjana. If I can't tell her what I hear, then there is no point in staying. Please give Mr. Tuttle my best."

I stood up. Not gracefully, because the damn couch was too low to the ground. But I got up and headed for the door. I had my hand on the doorknob before Jessup caved in.

"Of course you can tell Jorjana. Please sit down, Alana, and forgive my rudeness. It has been a long day."

We didn't like each other, but we didn't have to. I had made my point. He had made his. And since he'd apologized, I returned to my seat.

Jessup pulled a cell phone out of his pocket and dialed a number.

"Bring a Chardonnay for Mrs. Fox and Scotch and soda for me."

He pocketed the phone and leaned in, hands folded, making nice. I decided to at least hang around for the wine to arrive. No sense going thirsty.

"OK, I'm not happy that Lara insisted on bringing in new people. You, Jorjana, Alan Fox. I think there are too many getting into the inner circle. We like to run our campaigns with a small group calling the shots—it's easier to make adjustments when there are fewer players involved. But Ken has been impossible to handle lately. We've tried everything, believe me. So I'm willing to take the chance that you or Jorjana can get him back in line."

The door opened, and a guy dressed in a black dress shirt and black slacks entered. He carried two drinks on a silver tray. He put two linen cocktail napkins on the table between Jessup and me. Then he placed the wine within my reach and the Scotch and soda close to Jessup.

"Will there be anything else, sir?"

"Tell Mr. Tuttle that Mrs. Fox and I will be down for dinner shortly."

"Yes, sir." And off he went.

Jessup waited until the door closed before picking up his drink. I was two sips ahead of him by then.

"Here's what we need from you. Ken has to stick with the policies that we laid out for him. He can't change his mind, and he can't announce policy without consulting us first. Do you think you can get through to him?"

"Who's us?"

Jessup looked at me like I was standing on my head. "Graham, me, those guys downstairs. We put Ken in this race, and he needs to do what we tell him."

"Some of those other guys belong to the other party."

Jessup laughed out loud. "Of course they do. At least that's the party they support publicly. They would lose everything if it were known they are backing Ken Wheeler. You have to be careful of what you say in politics these days."

At first I was put off by Jessup's words, but I remembered that David Currie had been very careful not to be seen at the dinner for Ken. And when I thought about it, there was some truth to what Jessup said. Some opinions were not well tolerated in SoCal—especially among the Prius-driving vegan crowd and the tax-avoiding gated community crowd. Offence was so easily taken these days that it was getting difficult to have an intelligent conversation in public.

Jessup read my mind.

"Look, Ken is far from perfect. He has a short attention span. He worries too much about what is fair. But people love the guy. And he can bring people with opposing views together. I mean, look at that group downstairs. You've got guys from every corner of California supporting the same candidate. Imagine what Ken could do in Sacramento. He could make a difference if we can just keep him on topic. Now are you going to help us or not?"

I heard what Jessup said. Ken was a leader; Ken could compromise. All of that was well and good. That had nothing to do with why I was there. I was there to represent Jorjana.

"Mrs. York feels communication is unorganized," I said. "I will do what I can to get Ken's attention, but until you solve the communication problem, you are going to have a hard time keeping Ken on topic."

"Agreed. It's on the agenda. Graham wants this to be a working dinner. If you can help us keep Ken focused, we can get a lot done."

I expected him to say something nice to end our little chitchat, but he surprised me.

"I am going to take a chance and believe that you will keep what you hear between you and Mrs. York," Jessup said. "If one word leaks out, I know who to go after."

"Why aren't you having this conversation with the others?" I asked.

"I'm not worried about them, Alana." He was dead serious about that. I felt a shiver—and not because the room was cold.

"What are you going to do if I talk? Sue me?" I asked.

"Trust me, Alana, I have better ways of settling a score."

Of that I had no doubt.

Chapter Twenty-Two

My seat at the dining table put me squarely in the middle, facing the view. To my left was the movie guy. To my right was Alan. Graham and Ken sat at each end. Lara sat next to Ken, with her back to the view. Her phone remained on the table, face up.

The place settings led me to believe there would be five courses. I thanked my lucky stars that Jessup had let me out of his sight long enough to hit the loo.

The salads were already laid as we took our seats. It was a pretty presentation—butter lettuce with fresh tangerines, pomegranate seeds, and avocados. The bread plate held a lovely brioche bun and a tiny cup of butter. A goblet was filled with bubbly water and a sprig of mint. A server offered a Tuttle Estates Sauvignon Blanc to fill one of three wine glasses.

"Welcome, everyone." Graham raised his glass in a toast. "I hope you enjoy the meal. Nearly everything on tonight's menu is grown or raised right here on the property."

I took a sip of the wine. It was surprisingly light, with just the right amount of fruit. If the rest of the locally raised or grown meal followed suit, we would dine well.

"This is a working dinner, so let's get started," Graham said. "Greg, will you…"

Graham didn't get to finish. Ken Wheeler stood up and tapped his water goblet with a knife. I could tell from the clear chime that the goblet had not been purchased at Target.

"I have a few things to say, Graham."

The silence that followed seemed to suck all the air out of the room.

All the guys looked to Graham Tuttle like little boys looking to their daddy for clues on what to do. Lara glared at Ken, and I could see that she was trying to get his attention by pulling on his trousers. The servers stood stock-still out in the hallway. Jessup shot a look at me. I wasn't ready to step in, so I turned my attention to the wine.

"Not now, Ken." This from Graham.

"Yes, Graham. Now." Ken apparently did not hear the threat in Graham's tone or feel the tug on his pants. Or he didn't care. He put down the water goblet and stepped out of Lara's reach.

"Last night was a disaster. Thirty people were taken to the hospital, and our hostess remains hospitalized. Mac McDonald had guys with dogs all over the place, but no one thought to check the food? Where is Mac, by the way? I heard about the rhubarb in the salad from Alana. When was he going to tell me about that?"

Ken was the kind of guy who walked when he talked. He paced back and forth so fast I worried he would wear a hole in the cement floor. Jessup glared at me like this was my fault.

"You need to calm down, Ken," Graham said, the threat still in his voice. "We will go over all of that soon enough."

"We will go over it *now*, Graham!" Ken made it to Graham's end of the table in two strides.

"Take it easy, Wheeler." Jessup was on his feet and grabbed Ken's arm. Ken wrestled his arm back and pushed Jessup aside.

"Ken! Stop it!" Lara cried out. "Enough! Everyone, go back to your seats." Lara sounded like a grade school teacher reprimanding her students.

The look on Graham's face sent shivers through me.

Ken was the first to return to his seat. Jessup waited until Ken was seated to take his place. Graham didn't budge.

Lara glared at Ken and then, one by one, made eye contact with everyone at the table. When she looked at me, I could have sworn she looked a little surprised. Like she had forgotten I was there. She gave a small, regal nod to Graham. He finally sat down.

"This is getting us nowhere," Lara said. "We're all upset about what happened last night, but Graham has his best people looking into it. We will pray for Jorjana's complete recovery. She, thank goodness, is in the best possible hands. So let's focus on why we are here. Let's all take a deep breath and listen to Graham."

No one had touched their salads, but the servers swooped in and replaced them with a creamy leek-and-potato soup. Water goblets and my wine glass were refilled. Everyone very politely waited for Graham to pick up his soupspoon. He slurped down half of his soup before he had anything to say for himself.

"Lara, thank you for putting us all back in our place," Graham started. "Ken, you're right. You should have been informed as soon as our guys knew what was in the salad. Our lines of communication need to be streamlined, and we can hammer that out tonight. A lot has happened in the last twenty-four hours. Greg, will you fill us in on what you have learned?"

Greg was the assemblyman out of Stockton. He was a pudgy, middle-aged man who looked like he spent his days deciphering legal documents and pushing his glasses back up his nose. Greg pulled a piece of paper out of a folder and stood up. He turned toward Ken.

"Jesus Rodriquez is missing."

"Where is he?" Ken sounded alarmed. Lara may have paled a bit.

"Who is Jesus Rodriquez?" I asked.

"I'll get to that in a minute, Alana," Assemblyman Greg said. "Rodriquez left Stockton a few days ago. My guy is trying to track him down."

"Is his parole officer aware of this?" Lara asked. She was definitely paler. Any paler and her face would be the same color as her hair.

"His parole officer is aware of whatever we tell him," Greg said.

"Who's Jesus Rodriquez?" Me, again. This seemed to set off a flurry of other questions around the table. Graham Tuttle called for quiet.

"Jesus Rodriquez made threats against Ken, and we took it seriously. But obviously, we didn't do enough." Graham turned to Jessup. "Jack, tell everyone what we know about the breach in security."

Jessup waited to speak until the next course was served. The third course did not come from the Tuttle property. One exquisite scallop sat on a plate encircled by a curried aioli. The scallop had been seared perfectly—just brown on the outside and cool inside. I took the smallest bite I could, intending to savor the dish as long as possible.

"Our guys checked the background of everyone who came in contact with the food that was served last night. We know where every morsel came from, right down to the farm where the lettuce was grown. We have no reason to question the sources of the food. We do have reason to question the people who prepared it. It's no surprise that ninety percent of the caterer's workers are illegals."

"How can that be?" Ken looked right at me. "Jorjana swore everyone connected to the dinner was in the country legally."

"Everyone working *on* the York property *was* legal," Jessup said. "But the caterer runs a commercial kitchen in Santa Monica, and practically no one there is legal."

"Tell us what you think happened," Graham said darkly.

Jessup paused to make sure everyone was looking at him.

"We are looking into whether the driver who delivered the greens has any ties to Rodriquez."

Lara gasped. Ken looked grim.

"Somewhere between the commercial kitchen and the York place, someone put rhubarb in those greens," Jessup went on. "There's a good twenty miles between the two places, with plenty of spots for the driver to stop and let someone in the truck."

"You think Rodriquez is behind this?" Lara asked.

Jessup shrugged. "He made threats against Ken. Rhubarb ends up at a dinner where Ken is known to be. You do the math."

"You said you didn't know where Rodriquez was." Ken aimed this accusation at Assemblyman Greg.

"No, I said we knew where he wasn't," Greg responded. "Rodriquez isn't in Stockton."

"This is what happens when you let illegals run amok," Jessup said.

That comment brought silence to the table.

I ignored the pit growing in my stomach and took another tiny bite out of my luscious scallop. I sipped my wine and inventoried the looks on everyone's faces. It was pretty obvious to me that as disorganized as this group appeared, they were all united on the subject of illegals. Not a person in the room looked like they disagreed with Jessup's comments. Well, except me. But I sensed that no one was interested in my opinion.

"You know, I'm not sure Rodriquez was behind this," Ken said finally. "He doesn't know anyone in southern California. He's from San Jose, and all his contacts are there. Isn't that why he was paroled to Stockton? So he didn't hang out with his old gang?"

"He was paroled to Stockton so we could keep an eye on him," Assemblyman Greg said.

"That didn't work out so well, did it, Greg?" Ken asked. "Has your guy looked for Rodriquez in San Jose?"

Greg stiffened at that. He glanced at Jessup.

Jessup answered the question. His words came slowly and dripped with sarcasm.

"No, Ken. We haven't checked in San Jose. An attempt was made to harm you in Southern California. So we just assumed the guy who threatened you—and is no longer where we put him—might have gone to Los Angeles. But if you want us to waste time running around San Jose, then, fine, we'll look in San Jose."

Ken was on his feet again, pacing along the window. I savored the last bite of my lovely scallop and turned my attention to the wine.

"OK, let's say Rodriquez is in LA somewhere," Ken said. "I'm still struggling with the idea that he is behind this. Whoever planned this had to have connections in LA."

"You may recall that Rodriquez was incarcerated with dozens of men that hailed from all over California," Graham said. "Our prison system is nothing more than a fraternity for illegal gang members. Locking them up together just strengthens their bonds."

"What are the odds that a Mexican from San Jose wouldn't buddy up with a Mexican from Los Angeles?" Jessup's sarcasm snapped like a whip. "That's why we are looking into the driver of the catering truck."

Ken continued pacing and thinking out loud.

"Even if he did know someone, Rodriquez isn't the brightest guy on the block. Do you think he could come up with this plan on his own?"

"He's a criminal, Ken. The guy was convicted of a felony that involved dozens of people."

"Yeah, but we all know he had some help with that." Ken stopped pacing.

Jessup turned to face Ken so fast I thought his head would snap right off his neck. He was on his feet before you could say, "Shut up."

"That's enough, Ken." Jessup nodded in my direction.

Ken looked at me the same way Lara had earlier. Like he'd forgotten that I was there.

Ken put his hands up as if to surrender. "I'm just saying that we all know why Rodriquez has a grudge with me. But we also know he's not a smart guy. Are we sure he is the one who put the rhubarb in the salad?"

"We don't know where Rodriquez is," Jessup said, but his tone of voice made it clear that Ken was to keep quiet. "Graham's guys will find him soon enough, and then we will know if he was behind it."

"Let's concentrate on how to keep this campaign moving forward," the movie guy chimed in. "If Rodriquez is to blame, it will certainly add credence to our plans for immigration reform."

"Ken, you've been reluctant to follow our advice on illegals. Doesn't this convince you that current policies are ineffective and stronger policies must be put in place?" Graham asked.

"Rodriquez isn't illegal," Ken said. "His parents were, but he was born in San Jose."

"If his parents had been deported along with their rotten kid, we wouldn't have this problem," Jessup said.

More silence fell. And I was nearly out of wine.

Then Ken asked, "How much do the police know?"

My ears perked up at that. Weren't the cops investigating the same crime?

"I'll let Mac explain," Graham said. "Send McDonald in."

Mac McDonald entered the dining room like a dog with its tail between its legs. He looked like someone had beaten him with a leash, too. He stood at Ken's end of the table to address the group.

"Ken, I'm sorry I didn't answer your calls," Mac started. "Graham pulled me off your security so I could run down the leads we had. You've been in good hands. Graham only hires the best."

Mac then spent a lot of time elaborating on Jessup's theory of how rhubarb had made its way into the salad greens and syrup of ipecac had made its way into the dressing and onto the tables at the York Estate. A lot of the theory centered on this Rodriquez guy and speculation on how well connected he was to Mexican illegals in LA. According to Mac, everyone was focused on keeping illegal Mexicans armed with guns away from the dinner, and no one thought to question the veggies.

I refrained from pointing out that everyone's best intentions had done nothing to keep Jorjana safe because Mac's report bothered me. Mac didn't sound like he believed the story he was telling. I remembered Rusty saying something along those lines about the security for the dinner—that Mac didn't seem totally on board with Graham's demands. I wondered why Ken had no say in who was in charge of his security.

"We are cooperating with the police," Mac said. And turning to Ken, he said, "They haven't asked about Rodriquez, and we haven't brought it up. We are using every resource to locate the guy. We should have him soon."

"Thank you, Mac," Graham said. "Stick around in case we have more questions."

Mac stepped back, looking as miserable as a school kid wearing a dunce cap. He stood just behind Ken and leaned against the wall.

"Have we answered your questions, Ken?" Graham asked in a tone that suggested that discussion on this particular topic was over.

"I should have known Rodriquez had left Stockton as soon as you did," Ken said.

"Yes. I agree," Graham said. "Who has ideas on where to go from here?"

Everyone had an idea—and wasn't shy about voicing it. Many of the ideas focused on Ken's lack of focus. I'll admit to feeling just a bit smug that my original opinion of the Nitwit was shared by so many of his advisors. Still, Ken wasn't the only unorganized person in the campaign. From what I had heard, disorganization and poor communication were the campaign strategy. It was a wonder to me that Ken was the candidate at all.

I didn't bother adding my thoughts to the conversation. No one was going to listen to me—especially not Ken, who was busy arguing with every idea thrown at him.

Tomorrow I would advise Jorjana to stay as far away from this group as possible.

I decided to enjoy the view, since it was highly unlikely that I would ever see it again. With that in mind, I intended to take in every detail so I could casually mention those details when I needed to impress someone. *The last time I had dinner at Graham Tuttle's...*

It was full-on dark outside. The Malibu lights twinkled away and were joined by the stars. The lighting in the dining room was

low enough to not interfere with stargazing. I understood why
Graham Tuttle would build his house so damned far away from
civilization. You could see the whole universe from up here. Which
was likely appealing to a guy with millions of dollars worth of telescopes in his living room.

I entertained myself by trying to identify the constellations I
did know. I thought I saw the Big Dipper, and I was fairly certain
I saw Orion's Belt. I knew enough to know that Venus was a bright
light. I thought I spotted Venus rising just over the mountain. It
was a really bright thing, and it seemed to rise faster than the stars
around it. Or was that a plane?

The light was moving too fast to be a star. It had to be a plane.
The light grew brighter. I wondered if LAX had changed flight
patterns for some reason. Most planes flew to the north of Latigo
Canyon out of LAX. This one was flying due east and just south of
the canyon.

The conversation turned to how to prepare for debates. A
coach needed to be hired. Practice sessions had to be planned.
Policy had to be set once and for all, and damn it, Ken had to
follow the advice they were giving him. Voices rose. Someone
slammed a fist on the table.

The light took a sudden turn and headed straight for the
house. It was too small to be a plane, I realized. And it was flying
far too fast.

"Hey, Mac." I pointed out the window to the now fast approaching light.

Mac laid eyes on the light. In one swift move he grabbed Ken
by the arm and threw him to the floor. Mac fell on top of Ken and
yelled out, "Duck!"

Chapter Twenty-Three

The light exploded with enough power to shatter the window. The blast shook the walls and knocked the paintings to the floor. A brilliant white light—brighter than anything I had ever seen—lit up the dining room like a million flashbulbs.

My chair fell backward. My ears felt like they were bleeding. As much as they hurt, I couldn't hear anything. Not even my own screams.

I lay on the floor, still seated in my chair. I saw nothing but white, and I wondered if it was the storied white light you see when you die.

But I wasn't dead. My sense of smell was intact and working overtime. I smelled smoke and spilled wine. I felt panic around me as clearly as if I had all my senses intact. I closed my eyes. Still all white. I wasn't sure if I could move.

Someone pulled me upright as my eyes cleared. Shattered glassware and china covered the dining table. The picture window was gone. Smoke drifted out into the night sky. A guy dressed in a black T-shirt and black cargo pants had me in his arms. Seconds later we were in the hallway.

Another guy dressed in black held open a door and gestured wildly for my guy to hurry up. At least that is what I thought he was doing. I still couldn't hear. My guy descended a set of circular stairs. He said something when we reached the bottom. I still couldn't hear.

He put me down gently on something soft and held his hand up. I was to stay put. Then he put up one finger to indicate that he would be right back.

I had no intention of going anywhere. I rubbed my ears while I tried to get my bearings.

I sat on a couch at the foot of the spiral staircase. It was clear that I was underground. The walls around me were solid rock. There were no windows. The floors and ceiling were concrete. The room itself was spacious enough to hold two sitting areas and a dining table. A hallway sported a series of open doors and I saw comfy looking beds in each room. At the far end of the room, a kitchen lined the wall. The whole space was adequately lit and decorated for comfort. It felt safe. Which was all I cared about at the moment.

Graham Tuttle's other guests were scattered about the space, everyone wrapped in a blanket. The Silicon Valley guys lay sprawled on one couch. Alan sat in a recliner with his hands over his face. Jessup slumped in a chair with an ice bag on his head and blood dripping down his neck. Lara sat alone at the kitchen table, with her head in her hands.

I counted six huge guys in black T-shirts and black cargo pants milling around offering water and tending to injuries. These guys were even bigger than the Bunyans. One of the T-shirt guys knelt next to Jessup and wiped away the blood. He applied a thick dressing to the back of Jessup's head and wrapped it with a long white bandage. Then he stood there and applied pressure. Another T-shirt guy joined him and took notes on a pad of paper. Then the guy with the paper moved on to Lara and talked to her. I watched as he consulted with each of the guests, making notes each time.

Over in the kitchen, the two suits who had ushered me into the house paced back and forth behind a long counter like two lions in a cage. Flanking the counter were two T-shirt guys armed with rifles. Something told me the T-shirts were keeping the suits corralled.

My guy returned with water and a medical kit. I took a swig of the water, and my ears started ringing.

My guy wrapped a blanket around me and wiped my face with a cool, wet towel. He helped me slip my right arm out of my cardigan and put a blood pressure cuff over my bicep. He put a stethoscope in his ears. By the time he had my pressure read, I could hear again. My ears rang like the bell at recess, but I could definitely hear. I put my hands to my ears again.

"Is your hearing coming back, Mrs. Fox?"

I nodded.

"Good. Your blood pressure is one thirty over ninety. That's good, too."

"That's really high for me."

"You are in shock. I will check it again in a few minutes."

"What happened?"

"Someone launched a stun grenade into the dining room from a drone."

He said that as matter-of-factly as if he were reading a weather report.

The guy with the pad of paper joined us.

"Blood pressure is one thirty over ninety. Sight and hearing are coming back. She's lucid," my guy said. The other guy made notes and left.

"Who are you? Where am I?" Me, just needing clarification.

"You are in a safe room under the house," my guy said. "I'm part of Mr. Tuttle's security team."

I was just about to comment on how poorly Mr. Tuttle's security team protected him when Mr. Tuttle himself appeared. Ken Wheeler was at his heels.

"We have to call for help, Graham!" Ken was distressed. "Someone tried to blow us up!"

"It wasn't a bomb, it was a warning. If they wanted to blow us up, we would all be dead by now."

"Damn it, Graham! We need to call the cops!"

"For what? So they can crawl all over the house and tell us what we already know? My team is on it. They shot the drone down. They will trace it. No cops."

"But..." That was all Ken could come up with.

I felt his confusion. In my world, if someone shot a grenade at you, the first thing you did was dial 911. But then I looked around the safe room. This was not my world, now, was it? I wondered whom Graham Tuttle called if someone stole his car.

"You can't afford this kind of publicity now," Graham said. "First a poisoning and now this? Do you know what this will do to you in the polls?"

Ken didn't answer. His eyes went to Jessup and the blood that was now seeping out of his bandage.

The T-shirt taking notes handed his pad to Graham.

"Jessup is the only one that needs medical attention," Graham said as he read the notes. "My doctor is on his way here in the helicopter. He'll check everyone out and decide how to treat Jessup."

Lara got up then. Her hair was a mess. One sleeve of her blouse was torn away at the seam. As she stood, her balance seemed off. She took a deep breath. I watched her compose herself before joining Ken. She took her husband's arm and turned him toward her.

"Ken, listen to Graham. This is the way things are done."

"Lara, I don't like this," Ken said.

"I know, but it is best for the campaign."

Ken looked around the room. The Silicon Valley guys were on their feet. Alan lowered his hands. Everyone looked at Ken.

"Who agrees with Graham?" Ken asked.

All hands went up but mine.

"All right, then," Ken conceded. "We will do it Graham's way. No cops. But I'm not happy about it."

For once, Ken and I were in agreement on something.

Graham Tuttle's doctor arrived with a nurse in tow. He looked to be about ninety. She looked to be eighteen. He was bald. She had a full head of purple hair and a nose ring. One by one, each guest was led to a bedroom and examined. Not surprisingly, I was the last patient.

"Alana Fox, is it?" The doctor looked at the notes from the T-shirt. "Let's take your blood pressure, shall we?"

The nurse put the cuff over my cardigan and took the reading.

"One thirty over ninety, Doctor." The nurse released the pressure and busied herself packing the equipment away.

"Hmm. Let's look in your ears." The doctor stuck one of those plastic tubes in each of my ears. Judging from his breath, Graham had pulled him away from Happy Hour.

"Follow my finger." The doctor held his index finger up and swung it back and forth in front of me.

"Here is my private phone number. If you have any questions, call me. You may have some loss of hearing for a few days. You may see ghosts. This is all perfectly normal when recovering from a stun grenade. Remember, call me—only me. Do not report this to your regular doctor. Do you understand?"

I understood. I had no intention of following his orders, but I fully understood what he said. My regular doctor would pitch a fit if she knew my chronically low blood pressure was all the way up to one thirty over ninety. As soon as I could, I intended to call her office, if for no other reason than to get my hands on a medication that would prevent me from seeing ghosts.

Once the doc and his nurse left, we were ushered upstairs to the lounge. A bartender was on duty and quickly became the most popular guy in the house.

I gulped an ice-cold Chardonnay and stood in the hallway. I stood fast against the rock wall because it was a safe distance from the window. And I was pretty sure the Chardonnay would ward off ghosts.

The lounge was two steps down from my perch on the wall, which gave me a view of the guests—that was view enough. All of the guests, me included, had tidied up nicely using the toiletries in the safe room's bathrooms. Except for Jessup's bandaged head and Lara's torn sleeve, everyone looked like nothing extraordinary had happened.

The house had not fared as well. It smelled of smoke, and I heard the sound of drills from the vicinity of the dining room. I had no doubt that by daybreak, a new window would be installed, and all life in the house would carry on as if nothing had happened.

And then I wondered just how much money you had to have to not call 911 in an emergency. Jorjana had her own security team, and she called the cops if a coyote strayed onto the grounds.

Graham Tuttle appeared at my side. He had a Scotch in hand.

"I trust we don't have to worry about your discretion," he said.

"Jessup made it pretty clear that nothing was to leave the table," I said. But then, because I couldn't help myself, I added, "Does that still hold true if everything on the table was blown to smithereens?"

Graham didn't look at me. He took a sip of his Scotch and looked over the lounge. The guests were acting as if nothing had happened. I wondered if dinner would resume momentarily.

"You agree with Ken that the authorities should have been called?" Graham asked.

"Yes."

"I appreciate your honesty, Alana. None of these other clowns had the balls to question me. I hope you stay on with the advisory group. Ken needs you."

"No, thanks," I said. "I came tonight to take notes for Jorjana. I don't like what I saw, and I'm going to tell her that."

"Just Jorjana? No one else?"

"No one else," I lied.

Before Graham could respond, one of the T-shirts showed up.

"Mr. Tuttle, a couple of Malibu policemen are here."

That did not sit well with Graham.

"Who called the police?" His voice was loud enough to silence the guests. Everyone turned toward us.

"No one, sir." The T-shirt was quick to clarify. "They want to see Mr. and Mrs. Wheeler, sir."

Ken and Lara were seated on a couch. They rose in unison. Ken took Lara's hand.

"What's this about, Graham?" Ken asked.

"I have no idea. I thought we were all in agreement that we would handle this privately." Graham looked at Ken suspiciously.

"I didn't contact the police, Graham," Ken said.

"Shall we have them join us here, then?" Graham challenged.

"Please show them in," Ken said. His voice wavered the tiniest bit.

The T-shirt high-footed it away to grab the cops. I stuck by the rock wall, with one eye on the door that led to the safe room.

The T-shirt came back with two Malibu cops in uniform. I knew who they were—I had last seen them in my office, when they showed up to haul Maddie Sanchez back to her parents.

The cops recognized me, too. But if they were surprised to see me, they didn't show it.

Ken and Lara approached the cops hand in hand. The cops took a moment to assess the situation. I saw them eye Lara's torn sleeve. They saw Jessup's bandaged head. There was no way they could miss the smell of smoke in the house.

Lara barely took a breath. She gripped Ken's hand so tightly that her fingers turned white. Ken stood with his jaw set so hard you could have bounced a basketball off it.

"Mr. and Mrs. Wheeler, I am sorry to inform you that your son was shot this evening. He is in surgery at the Ventura Med Center. We are here to take you there as quickly as possible."

Lara went pale. She let out a small cry and fell into Ken. His arm went around her shoulders as he held her upright. Ken's eyes were closed. He shook from head to toe.

The suits were suddenly on each side of the Wheelers. One of them helped the couple to sit down. The other faced the cops and asked, "Which son? The Wheelers have three boys."

"I'm sorry, sir. It's Spencer. Spencer Wheeler, aged twenty-two."

Graham Tuttle and the rest of the guests gathered around Lara and Ken to offer comfort. The cops stood by, obviously uncomfortable with the situation.

Me? I stayed glued to the rock wall and wondered why Lara and Ken had not asked right away which one of their boys had been shot.

Chapter Twenty-Four

FRED

Fred and Wes spoke separately to the cops. It took longer than Fred thought was necessary, but the cops ran a check on his license and then called his former parole officer, who was as long-winded as anyone could be.

And Fred had to admit that he had not been as cooperative as he should have been. But his on-line research sparked from the articles in the Sacramento Bee had given him more information on Ken Wheeler than a regular guy should have. He probably should have told the cops up front that he recognized guy lying face down in the strawberry field as Ken Wheeler's son. And what with the confusion of the cops and the ambulance and then the medical helicopter, well, Fred wasn't thinking as clearly as he should have.

And then the cops found the gun in the truck.

Fortunately, Wes claimed the gun as his, and any idiot could see that a larger caliber weapon had shot the Wheeler kid. And Fred showed them how he and Wes had tracked the GPS device to find the stolen Mustang. And then wasted time explaining that the Mustang was still missing. The cops had no interest in the car.

The cops told them to show up the next morning to make formal statements at the station.

Fred figured that would give him enough time to sort a few things out. He had answered all the cops' questions truthfully, but he hadn't offered up what wasn't asked. When they asked him if he knew Spencer Wheeler, he did answer truthfully that he did not. They hadn't asked him if he knew who the kid was.

When Fred and Wes finally left the crime scene, it was well past dinnertime. Fred was surprised that he was famished.

"Where are the guys meeting again, Wes?"

"Over at the Ventura Bar and Grill. You hungry?"

"Yeah."

"Me too. Does that make us coldhearted?"

"No. It just makes us hungry."

"Let's go."

For once, Wes didn't have much to say. Fred was grateful for the time to think. He hated interacting with cops, and he really hated that his old parole officer had been called. Fred had been a model parolee, in his opinion, and he had paid his dues and put the past behind him. The last thing he wanted was that pinhead nosing around in his business again.

Fred felt real bad about the Wheeler kid. He had his theories of what had happened but couldn't tie some loose ends together. It bugged the crap out of him that he couldn't figure out what it was he was missing.

By the time Fred pulled into the parking lot at the Ventura Bar and Grill, Wes was out cold—sleeping off the aftermath of fainting. Fred took a minute to send a text to Alana. The cops were bound to tell her that he and Wes had found the Wheeler kid, but he didn't feel like explaining it all to her just then. He was still pissed that she hadn't called him as soon as the car went missing. The Mustang and the kid might both be safely home if he had known in time.

Fred gave Wes a gentle nudge to wake him.

"Hey, Wes. We're here, buddy."

"Oh, hey, yeah. Just dozed off for a second. We here?"

"Yep. Let's get a bite to eat."

The Ventura Bar and Grill was located in a strip mall in a part of Camarillo not known for its refinement. Behind the bar was a junkyard, and across the street was a pawnshop. The parking lot was packed with American muscle cars from the 1960s. The red Chevy truck, which stood out like a bad nose job in Malibu, blended right in here.

Fred and Wes walked into the bar and were greeted with a chorus of insults.

"Look who's gracing us with his presence! It's Lord Coveralls!"

"Hey, Wes, where'd ya get your boyfriend?"

"Whatcha drinking?" This from the bartender.

"I'll have a Bud," Wes said. The brew arrived in a nanosecond.

Fred looked hard at the beer. Lord knows he wanted one.

Wes noted the hesitation. "And a Coke," Wes said to the bartender.

The Coke arrived with a slice of lime.

"I know how you Malibu types are all la-di-da," the bartender grinned at Fred.

"And don't you forget it," Fred shot back. To Wes he said, "Thanks, buddy."

They joined a group of men sitting at a picnic table in the center of the room. The bar and grill wasn't much on fancy décor, but the place served up decent grub. While they waited on their burgers, Wes filled the guys in on the day's events.

The guys made sympathetic noises about the kid. But the car theft horrified them. Every guy around the table lusted after Alana Fox's Special Edition 1966 Aspen Gold Mustang.

"Where do you think it is, Fred?"

"Ya gotta do something—we're talkin' a '66 Mustang here!"

"Damn cops! Worthless pieces of…"

The burgers came. Fred added ketchup and mustard to his bun, as the talk around the table heated up. Fred let the group go on, while he tucked into his burger. He needed the guys to talk through the nonsense before he ran his theory by them. He took his last bite as the guys finally settled down.

"How did the GPS from the Mustang end up on the Wheeler kid?" someone finally asked.

"And what was he doing there?" asked someone else.

"Bingo!" Fred pointed his finger at the guys. "I have an idea. Listen up."

Fred wiped his hands on a paper napkin and pushed his plate away. The bartender brought another Coke, this time stuffed with six lime wedges. Wes signaled for another beer.

"When Wes told me about all the cars disappearing from the Central Valley, I did some checking around. I got a buddy who found out that Jesus Rodriquez got out of jail about two months before all the thefts started up. You all remember Jesus, right?"

The guys nodded. Jesus Rodriquez had run a gang that specialized in stealing vintage muscle cars.

"At first, I couldn't make the connection between Jesus and the missing cars because Jesus is from San Jose. But guess where he served his time? Folsom Prison. And guess who else is in Folsom? Diego Martinez."

"Holy crap! You think Rodriquez and Martinez decided to team up?" This from Wes.

Fred nodded. "Leave it to the wisdom of the court system to put two guys with similar interests in the same prison. It gets better. Guess where Jesus got paroled to? Stockton."

"Martinez is from Stockton!" Wes cried out.

The other guys nodded. The entire car world had breathed a sigh of relief when Diego Martinez was put away. The sentence was life plus thirty-two years, which everyone agreed was far too light.

"My buddy runs a website that tracks stolen cars," Fred continued. "He says that Martinez is still running his gang from prison by recruiting guys while they serve time. So Jesus spends eight years with Martinez and then gets paroled to Stockton—Martinez's turf. Ya can't make this stuff up."

The table went quiet. Every guy seated there had at least two vintage muscle cars, and the threat of losing them weighed heavily on their minds. The idea that Martinez could still run his gang made them all uneasy.

"That explains what's going on in the Central Valley," Wes said. "But Alana's Mustang was stolen from Malibu. How does the Wheeler kid fit into this?"

"Spencer Wheeler goes to UoP," Fred said. "That puts him and Rodriquez in the same town. I just can't figure out how they would run into each other."

"I know."

This from a guy at the far end of the table. His name was Eddie, and he had been oddly quiet through the whole discussion.

"I got a friend at the Stockton NASCAR track. He said the Wheeler kid was at the track all the time. The kid would bet on anything, and he got into big trouble owing a loan shark. Somebody paid off the debt, and then the kid ran home."

"You think the kid and Rodriquez met at the track?" Wes asked.

This latest news sparked more debate around the table.

"Where else would they run into each other? At the library?"

"What was Rodriquez doing at the track?"

"Looking for customers. Or cars to steal."

"Even if they did cross paths, would they hang out together? The Wheelers are rolling in dough. Rodriquez is a gangbanger. Doesn't make sense."

"But they met up today," Fred said.

"What makes you say that?"

"Because my guy says Jesus Rodriquez left Stockton this morning. I'm willing to bet he's the one who shot the kid and took the Mustang."

Chapter Twenty-five

The table went quiet. Eddie spoke first.

"Why do you think Rodriquez shot the kid?"

"Rodriquez rented a warehouse near the Port of Stockton last week. My buddy says he is stealing cars to sell to an Asian guy who doesn't ask questions. Apparently this Asian guy has a list of what he wants, and Rodriquez is stealing the cars and stashing them in the warehouse. My buddy thinks the cars are going to be shipped out on a container ship pretty soon."

"How does that put Rodriquez here?"

"The Asian guy wants a gold '66 Mustang. And I've got one missing."

"But the Wheeler kid…"

"I know the GPS from my Mustang was in the kid's hand, and somebody shot him. I'm guessing the kid stole the car, and when Rodriquez found the GPS, he shot the kid. Why the kid would steal the car is what I can't figure out."

"Does it have something to do with his dad?"

"You have to wonder, don't you?" Fred asked.

The guys called it a night shortly thereafter. Wes opted to get a ride home from Eddie.

"I'll swing by and pick up the 'Vette tomorrow, Fred."

Fred climbed back in the truck and headed toward home. He was beat—there was no doubt. But the missing Mustang and the mystery around the Wheeler kid and Rodriquez would prevent him from sleeping. He had some calls to make, and he needed access to his computer to make them. Fred hit the traffic jam on the 101 before he remembered the fifteen-car pileup. He sighed and told himself to use the time to reflect.

Tomorrow he had to make a formal statement to the cops. He wasn't looking forward to the conversation. He wondered if he should share his suspicions with them. Or would it look like he had too much information? The cops would definitely be suspicious if they found out he had known who the Wheeler kid was and had kept it from them.

Fred decided to keep his suspicions to himself. It wasn't like the cops had been at all helpful in tracking down the stolen Mustang. Served them right. Meanwhile, he had a car to find.

It seemed like hours before he exited the freeway. Hours he could have used tracking down the Mustang. He turned into the parking lot leading to the warehouse and braked to a hard stop.

The warehouse was located at the far end of a row of wholesale shops that supplied welders and plumbers and electricians. All lights were off in the shop windows, and the streetlights were dim. But Fred could see that the doors to the warehouse were wide open, and flashlights were dancing around inside. And in front of the warehouse sat a car transport truck. On the transport truck was Fred's favorite car—the 1948 Jaguar XK-120.

Fred's heart pounded so fast he feared it would fly out of his chest. He quickly turned off the headlights and put the truck in park. Then he shut off the engine. He sat still for a moment and counted backward from one hundred. He told himself that now, now more than ever, he had to keep his temper in check.

He never once thought about calling the cops.

He did, however, pull the gun out of the glove box and tuck it into his coveralls. He knew what was at stake if he used it.

It was a price he was willing to pay.

Fred let himself out of the truck and made his way behind the shops. He moved as silently as he could, listening as he approached the back door of the warehouse. He stopped outside the door and listened.

He heard two men's voices. He heard footsteps run up to his apartment and then back down. He heard the engine to the pink Porsche rev up. He heard the car rattle up the ramp to the transport truck.

"Thees one. Take thees one."

Footsteps ran up the stairs again. And ran back down in a hurry.

Fred cursed himself for labeling the keys on the pegboard so clearly.

He heard the engine to the 1956 convertible turn on. The cherry-red convertible with the custom red upholstery with white piping. The car without a scratch on it.

That was more than he could take. He pulled out the gun and put his key into the lock. Slowly, quietly, he opened the door to the warehouse. A Hispanic guy sat in the driver's seat of the convertible. His head was turned away from Fred as he backed the car out. Another guy stood by the transport truck shining a flashlight onto the ramp.

Fred stepped inside, intending to take the two men down or die trying.

It wasn't until Fred felt something bash in his head that he realized he had underestimated the number of thieves.

Chapter Twenty-Six

The cops stood their ground as the guests circled the Wheelers. Ken wrapped his wife in a bear hug. Jessup stayed seated in the lounge area, typing furiously on his phone. The T-shirts hovered about, keeping a safe distance from the cops. I didn't move from the wall.

"I will send the Wheelers in my helicopter," Graham Tuttle said. He pointed to two of the T-shirts. They sprinted to the front of the house. Within seconds, the sounds of whirring rotor blades were heard above.

The T-shirts returned and dissected the Wheelers from the other guests. Lara and Ken moved quickly but kept their arms around each other. I wasn't the only one who wiped away a tear as they left the house.

The cops were not happy with the situation. I could tell by how silently they stood and watched the scene unfold.

The pounding of drills and hammers continued from the dining room, drowning out the whirring of the helicopter as it flew away. The smell of smoke was strong. Jessup's bandaged head added to the overall sense that something more was amiss. You didn't need to be trained in espionage to figure out Graham Tuttle's dinner party had not gone smoothly.

Jessup finished his typing and stood up. He was unsteady on his feet, but his face held a look of determination. He stumbled his way over to the cops.

"We will take it from here, gentlemen." Jessup pointed to the door.

"What happened here?" The cops did not move.

"We have everything under control. Let me walk you out."

Jessup pointed to the front door. The gesture proved to be too much. Jessup's eyes rolled back, and his legs gave way. As he fell, blood burst through the bandage on his head. Jessup lay collapsed on the floor as a tsunami of red flooded Graham Tuttle's cement floor.

"Sir, sir!" One of the cops knelt down and tried to stop the blood flow.

"I need a medic unit..." The other cop was on his radio in a nanosecond.

Graham Tuttle made it to the cops faster than you can say NIMBY.

"He's fine! The doctor was just here! Cancel that call!"

The cops ignored him. The blood from Jessup's head poured out no matter how hard the cop applied pressure. The other cop relayed Jessup's condition into his radio, and the words he used were "nonresponsive" and "massive head wound." By the end of the conversation, the request for a medic unit had changed to a request for helicopter transport.

One of the T-shirts stepped up to Graham Tuttle.

"We have to let them send an ambulance, sir."

Graham Tuttle was displeased with that. He glared at Jessup. He turned to the T-shirt and growled, "Don't let anyone past this spot." And then he stomped away and disappeared up the stairs.

I stayed up against the wall. The hammering and drilling stopped. The only sound was the cop updating the dispatcher on Jessup's condition.

That condition got worse. He stopped breathing. The cop on the floor started mouth-to-mouth. The cop with the radio knelt down to keep the pressure on the head wound. I wondered why none of the T-shirts offered to help. They seemed pretty good with first aid down in the safe room. But they were lined up shoulder to shoulder, blocking the passage leading to the dining room.

I heard the chop-chop-chop of a helicopter yet again that night. The front door was closed, and none of Graham Tuttle's staff was anywhere in sight. Not a server or butler to be found. The T-shirts stayed glued together like toy soldiers.

I pulled myself off the wall and raced to the bamboo reception area at the front of the house. I pulled open the steel door just as two guys lifted a gurney up the steps. They didn't need directions on where to go.

I stayed propped against the door, and presently every cop in Malibu pulled into the drive. I wondered if they had rammed through the gate at the bottom of Graham Tuttle's property.

Jessup was wheeled out on the gurney with an oxygen mask strapped to his face. The guy didn't look great. His skin was gray. The veins in his hands were flat. He lay as still as the pillow under his head. The medics moved smoothly but not quickly—as if they knew their next stop would be the morgue.

"Mrs. Fox? We'd like to ask you a few questions?"

Sure. What the hell else did I have to do?

A cop led me to the same spot where I had stayed glued to the wall. I stood there and took a look around. Other cops divided the guests into separate areas and busily took statements. The T-shirts remained lined up, blocking the hallway.

Graham Tuttle returned from wherever he had gone. He shot a look at me that spoke volumes. I nodded at him and then turned and proceeded to answer every question the cop asked. I spilled everything from my conversation with Jessup to the exploding drone in less than five minutes. The cop wrote down everything I said and gave no indication whether he believed me or not.

Eventually the T-shirts left their posts blocking the hallway and let the cops spread out through the house. The guests finished their interviews and made their way out the open front door. From my spot on the wall, I saw a line of Range Rovers lined up to cart the guests away. Graham Tuttle had disappeared.

No one seemed overly concerned about me. It occurred to me that I had no ride home. I wondered if Graham had a spare Range Rover to lend me. I wondered if I was in the right frame of mind to drive. I could feel my heart pounding in my chest, and I wondered if that was how people with high blood pressure felt all the time. I wondered if it was too late at night to call my doctor.

I probably would have spent the night stuck to the rock wall if Stan Sanchez hadn't marched in through Graham Tuttle's front door. I've never been so relieved to see anyone in my life.

Stan wore the white shirt and jeans he'd had on at lunch. Over that he wore a leather jacket. The jacket did not cover his gun.

Stan wrapped his arms around me without saying a word. I held onto him as tightly as I could and buried my face in his neck. He felt warm and solid and safe.

"Pearson called me," Stan said, referring to the cop who had applied pressure to Jessup's head. "I'm taking you home."

He wasn't getting arguments from me. As we walked outside, one of Graham Tuttle's T-shirts appeared with my handbag and the pretty necklace David had found to complete my outfit. I reached for my neck. I hadn't realized the necklace was missing.

Stan's SUV was parked out front.

"Safe travels, Mrs. Fox," the T-shirt said before slamming the door shut.

"Are you OK?" Stan asked as soon as we rounded the corner, and the house was out of sight.

I hesitated. I hesitated because so much had happened, and all of it was outside my experience. I hardly knew where to start. So I started with the explosion, and once I got going, I couldn't stop.

Stan listened to it all without interrupting once. His jaw tightened when I said that Graham Tuttle refused to call 911, but he didn't seem surprised by anything I told him. Even the part about Spencer Wheeler.

"Strange things happen up in those mountains, Alana. Sometimes people live up there because they don't want our help. We'll find out who sent that drone, whether Tuttle likes it or not. And we'll find who shot Spencer. What were you doing at Graham Tuttle's place, anyway?"

That took a while to explain. The dinner seemed as if it had taken place months before instead of hours before. I felt like I was looking through fog at a distant memory. One detail remained clear, however.

"That group really hates illegal immigrants," I said.

"Yeah, Tuttle has a history there."

"What do you mean?"

"Graham Tuttle had a son who got involved with a Mexican girl when they were teenagers. The girl got pregnant, and Tuttle went ballistic. The girl's family was in the country illegally, and Tuttle managed to get them all deported. They ended up in some backwater village in Mexico, and when the girl went into labor, there were complications. Both the girl and the baby died, and then Tuttle's son committed suicide. He's been anti-immigrant ever since. That guy is a piece of work. If he had taken care of the girl, his son and grandchild would still be alive."

"How do you know this?"

"Just because Graham Tuttle doesn't want our help doesn't mean we know nothing about him."

There are definite advantages to having a cop in your life. Not the least of which is the access to data most folks never see. Not that I cared anymore about Graham Tuttle and his merry band of dysfunctional advisors. But that did clear up why he pushed Ken so hard to deport all the illegals.

We drove in silence for a while, giving my heart a chance to slow down and my head a chance to clear. I felt safe sitting next to Stan with my hand in his. I looked forward to a long, hot shower with Stan waiting for me in my bed. I needed to fall asleep in his arms. After a good night's sleep, I intended to show him how important he was to me. I planned on that activity taking until noon. I relaxed enough to knock down my blood pressure.

Stan took the turn toward my house and let go of my hand. And ruined everything.

"There's something you need to know, Alana. Spencer Wheeler was found by Fred."

"Fred? My Fred?"

"Yeah. He and a buddy were tracking the GPS on your Mustang? Which was stolen today?"

I nodded.

"You should have called me."

I nodded again. I should have called him. I couldn't remember why I hadn't.

Oh yeah, Stan brought Maddie to our lunch date, and I was irritated by that. It seemed petty now.

"So Fred tracked the GPS to a field in Camarillo," Stan said. "They found Spencer there with the GPS but not the car."

I rustled around in my bag and pulled out my phone. There was a text from Fred.

Call me in the morning, and I will explain everything.

I read it to Stan.

"What do you think he means by explaining everything?"

"Call him in the morning and find out."

It was well past midnight when Stan pulled up to my house. Apparently, it was not too late for company.

Standing outside my garage was David Currie. David held the duffel bag he used for overnight trips. He waved merrily like he was standing on the deck of a cruise ship as it left port.

"What's David doing here?" I asked Stan.

Stan turned to me, and I did not like the look on his face. I felt my blood pressure spike.

"I can't stay. I'm late for my shift as it is."

"But this is an emergency. I was almost blown up."

"Which is why every cop in town is on duty. I'm sorry, Alana, but I have to report in."

"But I need you."

"I called David and asked him to stay with you." Stan said it like that made everything better. "I don't think you should be alone tonight."

So much for shining knights in armor rescuing damsels in distress. I got out of the SUV without a word to Stan. I made certain to slam the door.

To David I said, "Don't say a word. Just get me a drink."

Chapter Twenty-Seven

David did as he was told. And then some. I took a criminally long, hot shower—the drought be damned—and went downstairs to find a pitcher of The Usual, along with a tray of cheese, crackers, and olives. David had lit a fire in the fireplace, and classical music played softly. My mail was stacked neatly on the sofa.

"Have a drink, darling."

David handed me a generous pour. I sank into the sofa and took a sip. Much to my surprise, I couldn't drink it. My throat felt as dry as the logs burning on the fire. My mind raced back to the smoke billowing out of Graham Tuttle's dining room.

"I think I should start with water, David."

"Of course, darling. Just a sec."

He returned in about a second with a glass of water. As I took the glass from his hands, I noticed the water was warm.

"Tepid water with honey, darling," David explained. "Your clothes smelled like smoke. This will help."

I took a sip. It did help.

"So, darling, do you want to tell me what happened now, or should I just cool my jets until morning?"

"What do you know?" I wasn't sure I had the energy to rehash the whole debacle.

"*Nothing*, darling. Stan was *frantic* when he called me. He said there had been an *incident* at Graham Tuttle's house, and one of his fellow officers called him and told him to go and get you. And then he was *hysterical* that he couldn't stay with you, so he called me, and here we are."

I had to smile. The idea of Stan being either frantic or hysterical was ridiculous. But I am well versed in David's embellishments, so I gathered that Stan had been pretty upset, which I found touching.

"Yeah, there was an incident, all right."

I rehashed the evening, starting with when I was sitting at the dining table and spotted the drone heading toward the house. As I told the story, I picked through my mail. David was struck silent as I spoke, which just reinforced how outlandish the evening had been. Bills, bills, invites, invites, bills. I'd just reached the part about the safe room under Graham Tuttle's house when I came upon a manila envelope. My name was misspelled on the front in very bad handwriting.

"What's this?" I wondered out loud. I put down the water and turned the envelope over.

"Very curious, darling. Open it."

"I know what this is," I said. "One of the paparazzi took a photo of me and said he would send it. I wonder why he didn't just e-mail it."

I pulled the photos out of the envelope. There sure were a lot of them.

"What is it, darling? You look like you saw a ghost!" David moved next to me on the sofa. "Darling, what does this mean?"

The photos were not taken from the parking lot of the Malibu Town Center. One showed me peering out the window of Jorjana's sitting room. Other shots showed the cars lined up the driveway leading to the Main House. Several were taken from over the pool and captured the chaos as Jorjana's guests fell ill. One caught me dragging Maddie toward the kitchen. I remembered Maddie saying she saw a drone flying around during the chaos at the dinner party.

"These are from the party last night," I said. "I wonder why he didn't give these to the cops."

The next shots were taken from the front of the house. Each photo was taken from a different angle, but together they told the story. Security guys racing in the house. Valets on their tail. The empty valet stand, with luxury cars parked just beyond. Then someone leaving the house.

"Isn't that Spencer Wheeler?" David asked.

The next shots clearly showed Spencer walking past the valet stand and to the cars. He reached into my Mustang. Then he looked at something in his hands. Next he reached back into the Mustang. Then he put the something in his pocket and walked back into the house.

"What was he doing?" I flipped back to Spencer staring at the thing in his hand.

"It looks to me like he was making an impression of your key, darling."

The next photos were taken above the parking lot outside the Malibu Town Center. Spencer stood next to my Mustang with his hand on the door. The next shot showed him behind the wheel as he drove the car away.

"Well, well, well. Look who got caught with his hand in the cookie jar," David said smugly. "I wonder what his daddy will say to him about this!"

David held up the photo and shook his head. Then he took a look at me.

"Good heavens, darling, what is that look for?"

"You don't know?"

My mind scrambled as I tried to remember who had been where and who knew what. My recap of the evening for David had ended at the safe room—before the Wheelers learned their son had been shot.

"Spencer was shot tonight," I said. I went on to fill David in on the arrival of the cops and how they had delivered the news.

"Oh no. Oh no." David looked crushed.

"But there's more," I said. "Stan told me that Fred was following a GPS on the Mustang, and he found Spencer."

David was speechless. Twice in one night had to be some kind of record.

"Why in the world would Spencer steal my car?" I asked. "Ken had already asked if I wanted to sell it."

David had nothing to offer.

"I need to talk to Fred," I said. I jumped up and made haste to the table in the hall where I store my phone. I dialed the number for the warehouse. The phone connected and rang. And rang. And rang.

"Dammit, Fred, answer the phone."

"Where could he be, darling? It's two thirty in the morning!" David was by my side.

"I have another number to try," I said. I ended the call to the warehouse and dialed 6 on my speed dial.

"Who's that?" David asked.

"Fred has a phone that he keeps with him at all times," I said. "It's the one rule I have for him. He has to be accessible when I call, no matter what."

The call connected and rang. And rang. And rang.

I hung up.

"Something's wrong," I said. "Fred always answers this line. I have to get to the warehouse. Can I take your car?"

"Shouldn't we call the police, darling?"

"And say what? Fred doesn't answer his phone?"

David considered that for a nanosecond.

"Grab your things, darling. I'll drive."

Chapter Twenty-Eight

FRED

Fred woke up from his bad dream and wondered why his pillow was so damn hard. Then he felt his hands tied behind his back and the tape over his mouth. It wasn't a bad dream. It was worse than that. The a-holes really were stealing the cars. And he was lying on his stomach on the floor of the garage with his hands and feet bound up tighter than a Thanksgiving turkey.

Fred knew enough to play dead. He kept his eyes half-closed and took stock of the situation.

He lay on concrete. His head, which was pounding like an SOB, was turned to his left. He could see the foot of the stairs leading to his apartment. His arms were uncomfortable but not in pain. His feet felt numb, but he could wiggle his toes. All in all, he wasn't in bad shape.

Fred figured he must have fallen when he got whacked on the head, and the a-holes just bound him up in place. He steadied his breathing and concentrated on what the thieves were up to. And where his gun was.

He heard the rackety-rack of another car being loaded on the transport truck. From the sounds of the engine, the a-holes had just loaded the hot-pink 1952 Porsche.

"You sure this one? She ugly!"

"It can be painted. It's not as ugly as that MG."

"Nooo, pink is worse."

As the a-holes argued over whether the '56 MG with its orange flames was uglier than the pink '52 Porsche, a third person tromped down the stairs from Fred's apartment. Fred shut his eyes and slowed his breathing.

"You guys done yet?" That was the third a-hole as he came down the stairs. The guy stopped at Fred's head.

"We got room for the Caddy. I'd love to have that baby."

"No, Jesus only wants those six," A-hole Number Three replied.

As he walked away, Fred heard the guy's sneakers squeak as he stepped onto the epoxy floor.

"We still have to change out the VINs and get back to Stockton before the ship leaves."

"It won't take me but an hour to change six VINs," A-hole Number Two said. "I really want that Caddy, and we got plenty of room."

"No, we gotta put the other cars on the truck too...Whoa!" A-hole Number Three stopped in his tracks.

"Whatsa matter?"

"Holy shit! Spencer got shot!"

"What?"

Fred heard the squeaks of sneakers.

"This just came up on my phone. Spencer was found shot in a field in Camarillo."

There was murmured conversation for a moment. Fred took a couple of deep breaths and opened his eyes. He adjusted his head ever so slightly. Across from the foot of the stairs hung a round antique mirror. Fred had found it on one of his treks to the Rose Bowl Flea Market. He had installed it in such a way that it reflected the cars on the floor so he could see them from the door of his upstairs apartment. He had done this to save his knees a nightly climb up and down the stairs before he went to bed. He thought of it as a baby monitor for his babies. But now the mirror gave him a glimpse of the a-holes as they moved their flashlights about.

A-holes One and Two were Hispanic. A-hole Three was a mangy-looking blond guy who really needed a decent shave. The three of them stared intently at a cell phone the blond guy held. The blond guy's lips moved as he read. One of the Hispanic guys looked to the other to read the news to him. All three of them looked as tense as piano strings.

"What about the Mustang?"

Blondie swiped his finger over the screen of the phone. "Nothing about the Mustang."

"Jesus popped 'im. I outta here." The guy turned and headed out of the garage.

Blondie and the other Hispanic looked at each other. Some silent exchange passed between them. Blondie put the phone away.

"We don't know what happened, Ceco," Blondie called after the guy.

Ceco turned around and glared at Blondie. "I not like Spencer ever. I not getting popped for this!" He waved his arms at the transport truck.

"We don't know what happened," Blondie repeated. "But do you want to cross Jesus now? With all you know?"

Ceco wavered.

"Before you get paid?" With this, Blondie convinced him.

Ceco spit out a barrage of Spanish that Fred figured was a reluctant agreement to stay the course.

"Get in the truck, then. We gotta go."

Ceco walked out of the mirror reflection. Fred heard the door to the transport truck open and shut. The other two guys turned their attention to Fred.

"What are we going to do about him?"

"Leave him there. Someone will find him soon enough," Blondie said.

"He's not dead, is he?"

"Naw, he's just old. I hit him hard enough he probably won't remember what happened."

The two of them found that hilarious.

Just then, the landline to the garage rang as loudly as an air horn. It shut the a-holes right up.

"Shit! What was that?"

"Let's get outta here!"

The a-holes turned on their heels and sprinted to the transport truck. Exhaust filled the warehouse as the truck pulled away. The landline stopped ringing. Fred waited. Sure enough, the second cell phone that was never out of his possession started vibrating. It was stored safely in a hidden pocket in his coveralls, and it shook like an 8.0 earthquake.

Fred closed his eyes and hoped like hell that Alana Fox had enough sense to know that something was terribly wrong.

Chapter Twenty-Nine

"Can't this thing go any faster?" I leaned over to see just how slowly David was driving.

"Darling, I'm going too fast already."

"Well, step on the gas or whatever makes this thing go. Fred is in trouble—I just know it."

David stepped on the accelerator, and his Tesla surged forward. Kanan Dume Road was devoid of streetlights. It was so dark outside it looked like we were driving into an abyss.

"What did Fred say again, darling?"

"I didn't talk to him. He sent a text saying he would explain everything in the morning."

"Do you think Fred knows why Spencer stole the Mustang?"

"I'll ask him when I see him."

David turned into the parking lot of the warehouse where I stored my cars. My 1954 Chevy truck sat at the entrance to the parking lot instead of safely parked in the garage under lock and key. Fred was as likely to leave one of the cars unattended in a parking lot as I was to adopt an orphan. If there had been any doubt in my mind that something was wrong, it vanished at the sight of the abandoned truck.

David stopped the Tesla next to the truck and shut off the engine. At least I think he shut the engine off. The car ran as silently as an owl in flight.

David and I both stared past the building supply businesses to my garage. Streetlights lent some illumination—enough to see that the big bay door was wide open. No lights were on.

"Now we must call the police, darling." David pulled out his phone.

"And tell them what? The door to the garage is open?"

I climbed out of the Tesla and closed the door as quietly as possible. I stood on my tiptoes and peered into the Chevy truck just in case Fred was taking a nap inside. The cab was empty.

I put my fingers to my lips and pointed to the back of the building. David put his phone away. As I snuck to the back, I heard his footsteps behind me.

The row of businesses backed up to open space. A chain-link fence ran the length of the building and kept the coyotes away. A narrow sidewalk led to back entrances. Each door along the way sported the name of the business behind it; there was a light above each door. The door leading to my warehouse was blank. And the light was out.

I slowed my pace as I approached. The door was ajar. I paused and listened. I heard nothing.

I pushed the door open with my foot. It creaked just the tiniest bit. At the sound of the creak, I heard something. Not a voice. Not a moan. More like a muffled cry. I peered inside and just made out a figure on the floor of the garage. It was Fred.

He lay on his stomach, his hands and feet bound in duct tape. There was more duct tape across his mouth. He looked pissed.

"Oh my goodness! Oh, darling! Oh no!" David burst into the garage like a mother goose protecting her goslings. It was David's nature to clean up messes, and he had Fred unbound and sitting up with a glass of water almost before I got the lights on.

The garage looked empty. I counted five cars left in the vast space. The open bay door looked like a wound. It was fairly obvious what had happened.

"*Now* can we call the police, darling? Oh, Fred, what's that on the back of your head?"

"The a-holes knocked me out. *Ouch!*" Fred touched the back of his head and winced.

"The police *and* an ambulance, then."

"We don't have time for the cops," Fred growled. "Those a-holes are hauling the cars to Stockton. I gotta stop them."

Fred got to his feet a lot faster than I would have thought possible. And then he raced up the stairs, taking two at a time. David and I followed.

Fred's apartment was a testament to the man's eclectic interests. On the walls of the tiny space, he displayed the treasures he'd collected from flea markets and estate sales. His collection of art deco prints covered nearly every inch of the walls.

But for once, Fred wasn't interested in boring me with the details of his collection. He went straight to his computer and sat down.

"Three guys broke in," Fred said as he waited for the thing to turn on. "They had a transport truck, and they knew exactly which cars they wanted. They're working for a guy named Jesus Rodriquez."

"Jesus Rodriquez!" I cried out. "That's the guy Ken Wheeler is worried about! They think he poisoned the salads!"

"What the hell are you talking about?" Fred muttered.

The screen lit up. Fred typed in something.

"Tonight, at Graham Tuttle's place…" I ran through the story once again.

Fred stopped typing long enough to give me a dirty look.

"Jesus Rodriquez didn't poison any damn salad. He's been too busy stealing cars up and down the Central Valley."

"But Graham Tuttle's guy said they didn't know where Rodriquez was. They think he's in LA."

Fred pulled up a new screen.

"Well, my buddy says Rodriquez checked in with his parole officer yesterday in Stockton."

"But Graham's guy said…"

"Graham's guy was lying."

"I don't know, Fred. Graham Tuttle is pretty well connected…"

Fred stopped typing again.

"Me and my guys all felt we needed to do something about all the cars getting stolen. The guy I know in Stockton started following Rodriquez three days ago. Rodriquez checked in with his parole officer yesterday morning. In Stockton. So he couldn't have poisoned your damn salads. The guy was in Stockton."

I didn't know what to say. I was confused by the stories told around Graham Tuttle's dining table and furious with myself for believing them.

"So who poisoned the salads?"

"I couldn't care less. Well, look at this." Fred pointed again to the screen. "Rodriquez left Stockton ten hours ago. My buddy thinks Rodriquez is on his way to pick up a new haul of stolen cars and bring them back to ship out of the Port of Stockton. After what I heard those a-holes saying, my buddy was right."

"Maybe we should call the cops now," I said. "And an ambulance, Fred. Your head looks awful."

The blue lump on the top of Fred's bald head looked like a colored Easter egg. He waved my suggestion away.

"No time for that. Those a-holes are going to load more cars on the transport truck and beat it out of town. I need to head them off. Look at this."

Fred pointed to the computer screen. On the screen was a street map with a blinking red light. The light was heading north on the 101.

"What is this?" I asked Fred.

"I put GPS tracking devices on all the cars," he said. "I can track them online. This is the one on the '48 Jag."

Fred switched to his e-mail, typed something quickly, and then pulled the app back up. Then he scribbled something on a piece of paper before standing up.

"Go ahead and call the cops, Alana," Fred said. "Show this to them. It's my user name and password for the app."

He stepped over to a file cabinet and pulled out several sheets of paper.

"Here's the list of VINs for each of the cars they stole and the license numbers and photos. The sooner you call the insurance company, the better."

Fred grabbed a jacket from a hook and headed out the door.

I thrust the paperwork into David's hands.

"What's this, darling?"

"Call the cops and the insurance company. Give me your car keys. I'm going with Fred."

Chapter Thirty

I caught up with Fred in the garage.

"Let's take David's car," I said.

"I'm going alone."

"No, you're taking me with you."

Fred stopped at the bay door.

"These guys aren't your society butterflies, Alana. You've got no business messing with them."

"They stole my cars, Fred, so I have plenty of business with them. Plus, you need me to keep you from doing something stupid."

Fred's jaw tightened. He knew I was right. He didn't like it, but he knew it was true.

He looked down the parking lot to where my '54 Chevy truck and David's Tesla were parked.

"Do you have David's keys?" Fred asked.

"Yup." I held up the keys and gave them a jingle.

Fred grabbed the keys.

"We'll take the Tesla. Damn thing doesn't make a sound."

Fred led the way to the car. He stopped just outside the car and pulled something out of his coveralls. It was a gun.

"What are you doing?" I cried out. "You're not supposed to have a gun!"

Fred held it out to me.

"It's not mine. The a-holes dropped it when they left."

He was lying.

"You said you wanted to keep me from doing something stupid," Fred reminded me.

"Yeah, but that didn't mean I wanted to do something stupid myself."

I took the gun from him anyway. And then I checked to make sure the safety was on. Knowledge about gun safety was yet another advantage to having a cop in my life.

We left the parking lot in silence—although it seemed like the gun at my feet was screaming at me.

Fred may be an expert on vintage cars, but he knew how to handle a modern all-electric vehicle, too. We were on the 101 heading north out of Calabasas in no time. Fred gave me his cell phone to track the GPS.

"We could probably plug this website into the car somehow," I said as I stared at the screen on the phone.

Fred grunted. "Probably. Do you know how?"

I admitted that I did not. The electronic dashboard on the Tesla was as different from my cars' rotary dials as the Mars Rover is from a horse and buggy. I found myself staring at the bright readouts.

"Pay attention to the phone," Fred said. "They aren't going to waste time loading up those other cars."

"I've only heard Graham Tuttle's story about Rodriquez," I said. "What do you know about him?"

"Rodriquez ran a gang out of San Jose about ten years back. They stole muscle cars and shipped them out of the country. To Asia mostly. That buddy of mine is convinced that Ken Wheeler hired Rodriquez to steal a '66 Mustang for him. It's kinda foggy how Wheeler ended up testifying against Rodriquez. My buddy thinks the cops were told to rewrite Wheeler's part in it because busting up the gang was the bigger fish."

No wonder Jessup had shushed Ken up so quickly. Everyone in the room except me—and maybe Alan—knew about Rodriquez. It didn't take me long to figure out who had told the cops to "rewrite" Ken's part. Lara said that Graham Tuttle and her father had planned for years to get Ken to run for office. A record of grand theft auto sure would have stifled that campaign.

"Who's this guy of yours that's following Rodriquez?"

"He runs a website that keeps track of stolen cars. He figured out that the increase in thefts coincided with Rodriquez getting out of jail. Rodriquez was paroled to Stockton. He served his time with a guy who runs a ring out of the prison. My buddy started following him to try to get enough evidence to get the cops to do something. Rodriquez just rented a warehouse near the port and is stashing cars there. My guy figures the cars will get shipped out on container ships."

I gasped.

"Alan was at Tuttle's place tonight. He said Graham was interested in properties the company has in Stockton."

"Let me guess. The properties are warehouses at the port."

I nodded. And I remembered something else.

"Graham said that he arranged for Rodriquez to be paroled to Stockton so he could keep an eye on him. He was certain that Rodriquez had poisoned the salads. They said Rodriquez was carrying out threats he had made to Ken Wheeler. Why would they lie about that?"

Fred was quiet, but I could see his mind spinning fast. When he spoke, it was in bullet points.

"Ken Wheeler testified against Rodriquez. Tuttle's guy gets Rodriquez paroled to Stockton to keep an eye on him. Spencer goes to UoP. Rodriquez threatens Wheeler. Tuttle buys warehouses at the port. How is all of this related? For one thing, I can't figure out how the Wheeler kid fits into this."

I had some news for Fred. I told him about the photos the paparazzo had sent to me.

Fred listened as he maneuvered through traffic. Even in the wee hours of the morning, the 101 was busy.

Fred paused as he changed lanes. "But why would Spencer steal the car in the first place?"

I had no answers there.

Chapter Thirty-One

"Take this exit and turn right."

Fred got off the freeway and stopped at the red light at the end of the exit.

He knew the way. "Of course. How stupid can I get? Give me the phone."

I handed it to him. He turned the app off before typing something into the phone. He slipped the phone into a pocket in his coveralls.

"You know where we're going?" I asked.

"Yeah. The a-holes are going to a chop shop that pretends it's a junkyard. I was just in that neighborhood. I should've thought of it."

"How do you know this?"

"It's my job to keep track of this stuff. That shop is notorious, but they haven't gotten busted 'cause they're careful."

"What are you going to do?"

"I'm going to go see what they are up to."

The light turned green, and Fred made a right. We drove until we reached a part of Camarillo unfamiliar to me. Fred seemed to know his way, though. He turned into a strip mall with potholes the size of bathtubs and parked. We sat outside an establishment called the Ventura Bar and Grill. I could smell fried onions inside the car.

"Follow me. Bring the gun."

I did as I was told. I rechecked the safety and stuck the gun in the back of my pants. Fred walked up to the door of the bar and grill and gave three sharp knocks. It opened immediately.

"This is Alana. She's with me," Fred said to the guy. "What you got?"

The guy who had opened the door was no spring chicken and looked like he had reached that age by taking the roughest road possible. He gave me a once-over before answering.

"The Mustang is there. They're backing the transport truck up now. It's dark, but you can see what's up."

"Thanks, Doug. I'll take it from here."

I followed Fred through the bar and grill. The place was empty and smelled like stale beer and fried onions. The floor was concrete, and the seating appeared to be picnic tables with benches. The inside was dim; the only lighting came from a string of lights over the bar. Fred walked right past the bar. Behind the bar was a set of stairs leading up. I figured my chances of snagging a cold Chardonnay were nil, so I followed him upstairs.

Fred reached the landing with me on his heels. The second floor was little more than an attic area littered with picnic benches and cardboard boxes. There was very little light, but a red exit sign hung on the far wall. Under the sign, I could just make out a door.

Fred opened the door and led me out onto a flat roof. Streetlights glowed over the parking lot. David's Tesla was the only vehicle there. On the backside of the building, a narrow alley ran the length of the strip mall. A chain-link fence separated the alley from a junkyard. A dirt road ended at the front gate of the junkyard, where a small structure stood. The structure looked to be little more than a metal storage shed, but it had a window, and a light shone inside. My 1966 Aspen Gold Mustang was parked outside. Next to it were two more vintage Mustangs.

A transport truck backed slowly toward the structure. Even in the dim light, I recognized my pink '52 Porsche on the top deck. There were five other cars loaded up on the truck. I didn't need daylight to know the cars were mine.

Fred put his fingers to his lips. We snuck around the perimeter of the roof before cutting back and ducking behind a huge HVAC unit. Fred got down on his hands and knees and crawled to the edge of the roof. I followed. Even from our position on our stomachs, we got a good view of the entrance to the junkyard.

A man stood at the end of the dirt road, giving directions to the driver of the truck. He was small in stature and wore a straw cowboy hat. His T-shirt was sleeveless, and every inch of his arms was covered in tattoos.

"That's Rodriquez," Fred whispered.

Jesus Rodriquez did not look like the kind of guy that would elicit concern from the likes of Graham Tuttle. Rodriquez looked like any Hispanic guy standing on any street corner in LA. And yet the guy was now taking possession of half of my cars.

"I'm calling the cops," I whispered to Fred.

"Just wait a minute," he whispered back. "The cops will have a better case if the truck is on the road with Rodriquez at the wheel."

The truck stopped, and the brakes settled with a sigh. The cab door opened, and three guys jumped out. Two of the guys were Hispanic; the third was a white guy with dirty-blond hair. They met Rodriquez at the back of the truck.

"We don't have time to change the VINs," Rodriquez said. "Let's get these Mustangs loaded up."

"Won't take me but a minute to change the VINs," the blond guy said. "We wouldn't want to get stopped and not have the VINs match the papers, now, would we?"

The three guys made a semicircle around Rodriquez. The blond guy looked cocky, like a sailor in charge of a mutiny.

"I said load up the Mustangs." Rodriquez stood his ground.

"Don't we have to wait for Spencer?" Blondie hooked his thumbs on his belt and smirked at Rodriquez.

"Spencer is none of your fucking business." Rodriquez took a step toward Blondie.

"But he is *my* business!" This came from the shadows.

From out of nowhere, Ken Wheeler appeared. He stood as still as a statue, fists clenched, barely breathing. But even from my perch on the roof, I could see the veins in his forehead pulsing hard.

"Why'd you shoot him?" Ken asked. "You wanted to get me. Why'd you shoot my son?"

"Hey, man, take it easy." Rodriquez raised both hands, as if to surrender. "What are you doing here, man?"

"I have his phone." Ken held up a cell phone in his fist. "I read the texts. He stole the car to protect me. Why did you go after my son?"

Tears flowed down Ken's face, and the hand holding the phone began to shake.

Rodriquez's back was to me. There was a gun tucked into the waistband of his pants.

"Because you went after me," Rodriquez spat out the words. I saw him straighten his shoulders. His arm moved slowly back toward the gun. "Your boy's an idiot. I told him if he got the Mustang for me, I wouldn't tell the world what you did to me. He believed me!"

Rodriquez nearly had his hand on the handle of the gun. "But he thought he was so smart and he put a tracking device on the car! He *was* gonna turn me in, just like his old man did! You rich bastards…"

Rodriquez never reached his gun. Four muffled pops sounded from the junkyard.

I started. Fred motioned for me to stay down.

One by one, Rodriquez, Blondie, and the two Hispanics fell face forward onto the dirt.

Ken looked at the phone in his hand as if it had fired the shots.

From the junkyard raced a group of men dressed in black T-shirts and pants. They held rifles. They carried backpacks. They surrounded the fallen men, with their rifles aimed at the men's heads.

"*No!* I said don't shoot!" Mac McDonald burst out of the storage shed.

He grabbed one of the T-shirts by the arm.

"What the hell have you done?"

"Just following orders, sir."

The T-shirts busied themselves wrapping up the bodies of the four men into tarps.

"But I said not to shoot!" Mac cried.

"We don't work for you, sir." The T-shirts worked fast. The four fallen men were wrapped up like burritos and hauled away.

"Mac, what have you done?" Ken came up behind Mac.

Mac spun around like a top. "Wheeler! What are you doing here?"

The two men faced each other, both obviously confused as hell. The T-shirts returned and busied themselves cleaning up the bloody dirt. Mac found his words first.

"We set Rodriquez up so he would leave Stockton and pick up these cars. We were going to tip off the cops. He would have gone away for good."

Ken grabbed Mac by the collar. "Rodriquez blackmailed Spencer to get to me. He shot my son!"

Mac shook himself out of Ken's grip as the T-shirts disappeared into the junkyard.

"You should have told me, Ken. I would have handled it."

"I didn't know until I looked at Spencer's phone."

Ken fell to his knees and sobbed.

Mac leaned over and took Ken's arm.

"Let's go. We'll talk about this later."

Suddenly the front of the junkyard was bathed in light. From behind the transport truck came a small army of men, all holding large flashlights and baseball bats. These men differed from the T-shirts like vintage teddy bears differ from GI Joes. They were in their sixties or older. They had beer bellies and gray beards. But they meant business.

"Don't go anywhere, buddy," one of them said. "The cops will want to have a word with you."

As if on cue, sirens sounded in the distance.

"Who are those guys?" I whispered to Fred.

He smiled as he pulled me to my feet. "I called in a few favors."
I heard footsteps behind us.
"Fancy meeting you here, Mrs. Fox."
I turned around and stared straight down the barrel of a gun.
Two Camarillo cops, guns drawn, faced me.
I knew who they were, too.
"Please put your hands up, Mrs. Fox."
I didn't say they were happy to see me.

Chapter Thirty-Two

FRED (THE CALABASAS GARAGE)

Two days after getting knocked out by the a-holes, Fred's head still hurt like an SOB. He wasn't sure if that was from the egg-sized lump on the back of his head or the hours he spent getting grilled by the cops. Between explaining how he found Spencer and how he witnessed four guys shot in cold blood, Fred figured he had spent more time in the last two days in the interrogation room than he had ever spent in jail. He was just glad it was over.

When he finally got around to seeing a doctor, Fred was relieved to learn he had a concussion and shouldn't drive for a few days. A few days by himself, tending to his babies, was just what Fred wanted most in the world. But then he got a call from Ken Wheeler. So now he had to prepare for company.

As he stood back and admired his handiwork, Wes arrived with a grocery bag in hand.

"Thanks for getting the cream and the blueberries, Wes," Fred said. "I had everything else."

"No problem," Wes said. "The table looks real nice. You sure know how to put out a spread."

In the middle of the garage, a table was set with a white linen tablecloth, sterling silver coffee pot, and English bone china cups and saucers. Sugar cubes lined up neatly in a sterling silver sugar bowl. A small pitcher awaited the cream. A crystal bowl awaited the blueberries. Linen tea napkins, silver teaspoons, and a plate of homemade biscotti rounded out the table setting. A semicircle of chairs was available in case anyone wanted to sit down.

The flower arrangement on the table was not to Fred's taste, but Ken and Lara Wheeler had sent it, so he felt he needed to put it on display. Just because he didn't feel like entertaining didn't excuse him from being considerate.

"I can stick around if you like," Wes offered as he eyed the biscotti. "I've never met a real live politician."

"Thanks, but I got this." Fred poured the cream into the pitcher and put the blueberries into the bowl. Strawberries would have looked nicer, but given where Spencer had been found, Fred felt it best to go with blueberries. Not that he expected the Wheelers to actually eat anything.

"Call me if you need me," Wes said.

As Wes drove away in his beloved Corvette, a black Cadillac Escalade arrived. Fred double-checked that the table was perfect and then went to greet his guests.

Ken and Lara Wheeler emerged from the Escalade after their driver opened the door. The Wheelers looked like shrunken versions of their former selves. Lara's face was pale. Ken looked lost, like he had wandered into a strange world and couldn't find his way out.

Behind Ken and Lara came the Wheeler boys. Todd and Evan bounced out before turning to offer a hand to their older brother.

Spencer Wheeler moved as slowly as a ninety-year-old. His right arm was wrapped in a sling. A line of stitches ran down his face, and his eyes were nearly swollen shut. His face was the color of the blueberries. His brothers handled him like he was made of blown glass.

Fred knew that a bullet had torn its way through Spender's back and out his shoulder. Rodriquez had shot the kid after beating him to a bloody pulp. Shot him as he lay on the ground. Either Spencer was the luckiest kid alive, or Rodriquez was the world's worst shot.

Fred only knew this because Alana told him. It wasn't as if there had been anything reported in the local news about it. Hardly a word. The official news reports on Spencer's injuries were attributed to target shooting gone awry. The Wheelers had asked for, and been given, remarkable privacy.

"Fred, thank you for taking the time to see us." Ken put out his hand.

"Yes, Fred, thank you," Lara echoed.

Fred shook Ken's hand. It took Fred aback when he had to look up to meet Ken's gaze. Fred was used to being the tallest guy in the room. But the Wheeler men all towered over him. Fred's unease jumped up a notch.

"Alana is on her way," Fred told them. And then, to distract himself from his unease, he asked, "Would you like some coffee, Mrs. Wheeler? Do you want to sit down, Spencer? Would you like to see the cars, Mr. Wheeler?"

Yes, yes, and yes.

Fred led the way into the garage. Lara busied herself pouring coffee. Todd and Evan settled Spencer into a chair. Ken wandered over to the '48 Jaguar.

"Now that is a nice car," Ken said quietly. "With the wood frame, too. Is that the original color?"

"Original everything. Only has fifteen hundred miles on her."

Fred and Ken discussed the virtues of the Jag as Lara sipped her coffee. Todd and Evan fussed over Spencer. In due time, Alana arrived.

Alana drove the '52 hot-pink Porsche. After the meeting, she would leave it in the garage and take another car. After the events in Camarillo, Alana had expressed a desire to repaint the Porsche. Something about how the bright paint would always remind her of the execution they had witnessed. Whatever. Fred made the appointment to get the Porsche painted before she could change her mind. He ordered paint in a cream color without consulting her.

Alana made her way to Lara, and the two women exchanged hugs. Todd and Evan shook her hand. Spencer stayed seated. Fred closed the hood on the Jag, and he and Ken joined the others.

Everyone inquired about the health of everyone else. They all lied and said they were fine. Lara beat back tears, and Ken looked like it took an effort for him to just draw a breath. Spencer sighed. Todd and Evan attacked the biscotti.

Alana looked at the coffee in her cup with disappointment. Fred knew she would have preferred a drink.

Ken got things moving.

"Lara and the boys and I want you to know that we are sorry for what you went through. Alana, Fred, we are indebted to you forever."

Fred knew this was the part where polite society people would say, "Aw, shucks, it was nothing," but he wasn't a polite society kind of guy. So he kept his mouth shut. He noticed Alana didn't say anything, either.

Ken paused. He seemed to shrink two sizes.

"I want you to know the truth. Not the story that was polished and rewritten for public display."

Fred thought about the one flimsy report that had made the news—a buried story about a shooting incident in Camarillo that came and went like lightning. The murdered men were referred to as felons on the run. Ken's name never made it into the story. Nor had the stolen Mustang and Spencer's part in all of that. The only news about the Wheeler family was that Ken was taking time off the campaign trail while Spencer recuperated from his accident. Fred was surprised they didn't chalk Spencer's injuries up to a skateboard accident.

Ken began to pace.

"About ten years ago I bought a '66 Mustang from Jesus Rodriquez. I wanted that car so badly I didn't ask all the questions I should have."

Ken stopped pacing and looked at Alana.

"It was wrong to get involved with Rodriquez, and I knew it. To make things worse, I put Rodriquez in touch with other car collectors I knew."

Ken went back to pacing.

"Anyway, the police got involved, and to save my own hide, I helped them catch Rodriquez. At the same time, I had to explain to the other collectors that the guy I'd put them in touch with was a crook. It didn't go over very well, as you can imagine, but life went on. Everyone knows these things happen.

"So, I testified against Rodriquez, and he was found guilty. Rodriquez made all kinds of threats in the courtroom after he was sentenced. But I didn't take him seriously…"

"None of us did," Lara interrupted. "We dismissed him as a criminal not worthy of our attention. Maybe if we had been more compassionate, none of this would have happened."

Ken stopped pacing and faced his wife.

"This is on me, Lara. I put my family and friends in danger. I take the responsibility."

Ken and Lara looked at Spencer. Fred was certain he saw them flinch.

"I sold my company soon after that." Ken went back to the pacing. "About a year ago, the party leaders approached me about running for governor. We thought it was a good idea." Ken nodded in Lara's direction.

"Graham offered to help," Lara said. "We thought having a supporter in Southern California would be to our advantage."

"But he took advantage of us." This from Spencer.

Everyone turned to look at him. Spencer struggled to his feet. He waved his brothers' helping hands away.

"This is my fault," Spencer said. "I acted like a spoiled brat—a rich, entitled, spoiled brat spending all my days at the track instead of in school. I ended up owing the wrong kind of guy a lot of money. Jack Jessup paid the guy off, and then he told me to leave school and help with Dad's campaign."

Spencer looked Alana straight in the eye.

"Mom and Dad didn't know about it. Graham didn't tell them until Dad started arguing with Graham about how to run his campaign."

"Spence, take it easy." Ken put his arm around his son. "Sit down, son. You need to rest."

Ken eased the kid back into the chair. He stayed there with one hand on the kid's good shoulder.

"Graham Tuttle's hand is in every part of this. He did step up and offer to help with the campaign. It seemed too good to be true…not unlike my association with Rodriquez…I should have followed my gut, but I didn't. Before I knew it, Graham had all these advisors weighing in on what my platform would be. I started to feel like a puppet, and I told Graham I didn't like the way things were going. He accused me of being a flake. That's when he brought up Jesus Rodriquez. And the trouble that Spencer was in,"

Ken paused and looked at his wife.

"We've since learned that Graham arranged for Jesus to be paroled to Stockton, where he had people that could keep an eye on him," Lara explained. "Graham knew about Ken's involvement with Jesus, and he was worried that Jesus would go to the press with crazy accusations. Ken is well liked among the voters, but you know how eager the press is these days to believe anything sinister. Graham wanted Jesus out of the way, so he used his dark connections to convince Jesus to start stealing cars again. Graham went as far as to provide warehouse space near the Port of Stockton so Jesus could store stolen cars before shipping them overseas to Asia."

Alana gasped loud enough to catch Lara's attention. Alana shook her head and motioned for Lara to go on.

"Graham is very persuasive," Lara went on. "He convinced us that Ken was in danger and that Jesus was the threat."

"There's more," Ken said. "Graham's intention was to get Rodriquez arrested again and send him away for a good long time. That plan may have worked, but then Rodriquez went after Spencer."

"Let me tell the rest of it, Dad," Spencer said.

The kid got up and faced Alana. He towered over her physically, but he looked like a little boy caught with his hand in the candy jar.

"A lot of things happened at once, and it was really confusing, Mrs. Fox," Spencer began. "I'm not making excuses, but I was in over my head. I ended up owing a guy a bunch of money—more than I could get my hands on. Then, out of nowhere, Jack Jessup showed up at my dorm and said he would pay the debt. I still don't know how he found out. He insisted that I tell him about everyone I'd met at the track. I'd met some shady characters, for sure—Jesus Rodriquez was one of them. Mr. Jessup told me to leave Stockton but to let him know if Jesus ever tried to get ahold of me. But I couldn't tell my parents."

Spencer turned to his folks. It was hard to tell through the bruises, but the kid did look repentant.

"Just before we all came down to Malibu, Jesus sent me an e-mail and said that he was going to tell a reporter a bunch of lies about my dad and me unless I helped him out. I panicked, but I called Mr. Jessup. He said to go along with whatever Jesus told me to do. He said he plans for Jesus. That's why I ended up taking your car, Mrs. Fox."

Fred noticed the use of the word "taking," not "stealing." Like the kid was going to return the car the next day or something.

"Jesus was looking for vintage Mustangs," Spencer said. "I sent him photos of yours, and he told me to get it. He said that was all I had to do and he wouldn't tell the reporter anything, Mr. Jessup told me to stall Jesus as long as I could."

Alana sank down into a chair with a dazed expression on her face.

"Mr. Jessup gave me a kit to make an impression of the key for the Mustang. Then all I had to do was find a time to take the car. I felt really bad about it, Mrs. Fox. Especially when you were so nice to let me drive it."

Fred really wished he had a drink for Alana.

"I took the car to the spot where Jesus said to meet," Spencer said. "I thought that was it. And then Jesus found the GPS."

The silence in the garage came in many forms. Ken and Lara fought back tears. Todd and Evan stopped downing biscotti. Alana looked like she could kill Spencer. Fred counted backward from one hundred.

Alana spoke first. "Does anyone know where Graham is?"

Fred pondered the Wheeler family's story. Yes, Graham Tuttle's fingerprints were all over everything, but the billionaire himself had not been seen in seventy-two hours.

"The police are still searching for him," Ken said. "Not surprisingly, his staff claims to know nothing about his whereabouts."

"What about the bodies of the guys who were killed?"

"No sign of them either."

"What about Mac McDonald?"

"He isn't talking."

"Why not?"

"I suspect Graham has some kind of control over Mac, even in absentia."

"We saw four guys murdered!" Alana said.

"Yes, but there are no bodies. And no one has reported those four men missing."

"Tuttle's going to get away with it, isn't he?" Fred said.

Ken didn't answer the question. He had more bad news.

"Jack Jessup died this morning."

Alana gasped.

"You're not surprised, are you?" Ken asked. "It was not in Graham's best interests for Jack to live."

"You think he had Jessup killed?" Alana asked. "No, that can't be. Jessup was in really bad shape when he was airlifted out."

"Bu the doctors thought they could save him," Ken said. "I think it is suspicious that twenty-four hours after the doctor said he would recover, the guy is dead."

Alana looked like she needed a drink.

"I think Jessup knew too much," Ken went on. "And Graham has too much to lose. Graham took desperate measures to get me in line—including the lengths he went to convince me that Rodriquez was a threat to me. I told the police to check out the crops that Graham is growing on his property. I suspect that the rhubarb came from Graham's farm."

"But Jessup said they checked out where the food came from," Alana said.

"He said they knew where every morsel of food came from," Ken said. "He didn't tell us where those farms were."

"But why would they do that?"

"Graham wanted to scare me. Graham has a vendetta against immigrants and needed to convince me that they are dangerous. What better way than to say Rodriquez had poisoned the salad? I suspect they were behind the drone attack, too."

"But they could have killed you," she said.

"Again, I think the intention was to instill fear. They loaded it with a stun grenade because they figured no one would get seriously hurt."

"Except Jessup."

"Jessup had the bad luck to hit his head on the edge of the table."

"How are you going to prove all of this, Ken?"

"I can hire lawyers just as fast as Graham can disappear. And detectives to find him. When I do find Graham, the first question I'm going to ask him is how a drone was able to shoot a grenade through the window of a house that is fortified like a bunker. That window shattered far too easily."

Alana paled. The egg on the back of Fred's head throbbed.

Fred was about at the end of his good manners. He'd kept his mouth shut and counted backward so many times since the Wheelers arrived, he was sure he'd counted down from a million. Everything the Wheelers said only verified Fred's opinion of rich people—they took advantage, adjusted the laws to suit themselves, and then got away with it. Every damn time. He just hoped the family would leave soon.

Ken wasn't done, though. He turned to Fred.

"Fred, I want to repay you for everything you endured. Alana told me a little bit about your past. I have a friend in Sacramento who I am certain can erase the felony conviction on your record. Do I have your permission to look into it?"

Fred was taken aback. But he managed a small nod. And then wondered if he was selling out.

"Very well then. It seems to me it could be argued that you have paid your dues. The other guy did fully recover, didn't he?"

Fred nodded again. The other guy had not only recovered, he had delivered cream and blueberries that morning.

"Very well. I will take care of it." Ken looked at his watch and then at his family. "We have a plane to catch."

Fred managed a "thank you."

Within moments, the Wheeler family loaded themselves back into the Escalade and away they went.

"I wonder what time their flight is," Fred said, because he didn't know what else to say. "Traffic to LAX is going to be a mess."

"They're taking a private jet out of the Camarillo airport," Alana replied.

Of course they were.

Rich people.

Chapter Thirty-Three

"The Porsche is going into the shop tomorrow for the new paint job," Fred said. "I'm having it painted cream. It's probably going to take more than one coat."

I handed him the keys to the 1952 Porsche convertible. I was not surprised that covering up the car's current hot-pink exterior would take some doing. I was surprised that I didn't care what the new color would be. I just wanted to stop thinking about witnessing four men being shot dead as the pink Porsche shone merrily from the top of a transport truck.

"Which car are you going to take?" Fred asked.

I looked around the garage. Not the red '48 Jaguar or the cherry-red '56 Thunderbird or the red '54 Chevy truck. Why were so many of my cars the color of blood?

Definitely not the '66 Mustang.

The '56 MG was just too loud, with those orange flames on the side—what was I thinking when I ordered that?

Which reminded me of something.

"Fred, Tori is pregnant again."

Fred paled.

"Paint the MG a pretty dark blue."

Fred blinked.

My eyes landed on the yellow 1957 Chevy Bel Air. The one big enough to install a hot tub in it.

"And while you're at it, paint the Bel Air cream, too. Tori's having twins."

Fred sighed.

I was surprised that my orders to repaint the cars did not give me the nasty satisfaction that I usually got. I was too weary to wonder why.

That took care of the paint jobs, but I still needed a car to drive. I considered the '56 Plymouth Fury. The Fury was white with a pretty gold trim. There was just one problem with it.

"Does the Fury make right turns yet?" I asked Fred.

"Yeah. I made the repairs. She drives like a dream. I'll get the keys."

Five minutes later I was on the road and heading back to Malibu for a lunch date with Stan.

I felt like I had aged ten years in the last few days. The drama of dealing with Ken Wheeler, of Jorjana fighting for her life, of getting blasted from a stun grenade, of finding Fred tied up and my cars stolen and then watching Graham Tuttle's men kill Jesus Rodriquez and the others was hard to get over. And the fact that it had all happened within forty-eight hours was, well, more than I really cared to think about.

I wanted nothing more than to return to my calm, organized life of arranging social introductions and attending parties. Going forward, I intended to avoid politics and politicians the way I avoided Beverly Hills. I was getting too old to mix with that kind of riffraff.

The first step on my path to bringing order to my life started with Stan. As I parked the Fury outside Taverna Tony, I felt calmer than I had felt in days. Everything would fall into place as soon as I talked to Stan.

Once again, I arrived first. As the hostess led me to my favorite table, who should sit in my path but Alan and Little Miss Tight Buns. And their entire flock of children.

Their table looked like the chef had tossed the food at them instead of serving it on plates. Hummus was spread like finger paint; pita bread was torn into fragments and strewn from one end of the table to the other. The youngest kid sat in a high chair and fingered angel hair pasta like it was Play-Doh. LMTB offered a dolma to the middle kid, who pursed her lips and shook her head. The oldest child waved a lamb kebab around like he was conducting an orchestra. Alan sat at the head of the table and surveyed the scene. The look on his face stopped me dead in my tracks.

He was enjoying himself.

Not once in the twenty years that Alan Fox and I had been married did I ever see the man so content. I had seen him happy. I had seen him upset. I had even seen him delirious over the close of a big deal. But never had I seen him as relaxed and pleased as he looked at that moment.

As I looked at Alan and his family, I realized that he was in heaven being a father to all those kids. The noise and the mess were my worst nightmare, but to Alan, it was a dream come true.

You can say a lot of things about me, and most of them would be true. But I do know when to fight a battle and when to let go. It was time to let my anger with Alan go.

That was the moment I forgave him for divorcing me.

"Alan! Tori!" I swooped in before I had second thoughts.

"Why, hello, Alana," Alan said as he got to his feet. "How are you? How is Jorjana?"

Alan put his hand out. I ignored it and gave him a hug. The look on his face was priceless.

Tori put the dolmas down and stood up with effort. She wore shorts and a maternity top decorated with tzatziki dip. I hugged her anyway.

"How *is* Jorjana? We've been worried," Tori asked. She kept her hands on my arms. It occurred to me that it was the first time we had ever touched. Usually I kept myself at least an arm's length away for safety reasons. Hers, not mine.

"She is recovering. It is slow, as you might expect," I said. "There were concerns about her kidney function, and they are monitoring her to make sure she doesn't get pneumonia, but she is out of the woods."

"That's good to hear."

I responded like a grown-up for a change.

"Tori, thank you for your help the night of the dinner," I said. "You were amazing. Jorjana might not have made it if you hadn't discovered her."

"Well, Jorjana's staff is pretty amazing, too. She was in good hands."

Alan's mouth may have dropped open about then.

"Alana, I don't think you have met all of our children," Tori said as she turned to the kids. "You know Chaucer, of course, and this is our daughter, Guinevere, and our youngest, Palamon."

The kids looked at me upon hearing their names. Chaucer frowned like he was trying to remember where he had seen me before. Well, it had been a while. And then there was the restraining order. But that was another story.

"You do have your hands full," I said.

"Yes, and five kids will be even busier," Tori said. And then she went and ruined the moment. "Of course, it would help if we could afford to hire more help."

I knew where she was heading—down the path to why-does-Alana-get-so-much-money land. Well, I wasn't going there. The money Alan paid me was none of her damn business. I considered the alimony more like residual payments. I built the business that Alan ran, and I was entitled to the profits. I bit back the nasty retort on the tip of my tongue and continued to play nice.

"I'll let you get back to your lunch," I said to Alan. "Good seeing you. Both of you."

I left Tori to deal with the messy kids and Alan to wonder if hell had frozen over.

I settled into my favorite table on the landing and rewarded myself for my good behavior with a glass of Chardonnay. I was on the second glass when Stan finally showed.

He wore jeans, sandals, and a blue shirt with the sleeves rolled up. He looked relaxed and was so handsome it almost hurt to look at him. He smelled good, too—like soap and sandalwood cologne. I held onto his hug an extra long time.

"Did you finally get enough sleep?" Stan asked as he sat down.

"I did. Fourteen hours. I feel better but I'll probably sleep another fourteen tonight."

"You look rested. How did the meeting with the Wheelers go?"

I told him. He held my hand as I relayed Ken's theory of Graham Tuttle's involvement in the poisoned salad and the drone attack. He frowned when he heard of Jack Jessup's death. Stan did all of that even as his phone buzzed away in his jeans pocket.

"Do you need to answer that?" I asked him.

"No. I'm here with you." He looked me straight in the eye and smiled. But it was obvious he was dying to answer the phone.

The guy was trying. I gave him that. So I cut him some slack.

"Go ahead—answer it."

He pulled the phone out of his pocket and stared hard at the screen. His relief was so obvious that I could practically smell it.

"No worries. This can wait." He pocketed the phone and smiled at me.

"How's Jorjana?"

And that was when I knew he had not heard a word I'd said. Stan was a cop through and through. He lived by the law. He risked his life to enforce it. Stan Sanchez did not hear that someone arranged to poison a group of citizens, shoot a grenade into a dinner party, and order four men shot in cold blood and then change the subject. For all the hand-holding and smiling, Stan's mind was somewhere else.

Whether the somewhere else was his kids or his job didn't matter. He wasn't fully with me. And that did not sit well with me.

"Jorjana is recovering," I said. "She'll stay in the hospital until the doctors are certain she won't develop pneumonia. If all goes well, she will be home in a few days."

The waitress came to get our order.

Stan's jeans started buzzing again.

"Can you give us a few minutes?" I asked her.

Then to Stan I said, "We need to talk."

Chapter Thirty-Four

"Darling, are you warm enough? Should I fetch another blanket?"

Jorjana waved David away.

"I am quite comfortable. Please stop fussing over me."

"You almost *died*, darling! And the doctor said to keep a watch out for signs of pneumonia!"

Jorjana, David, and I relaxed by the pool at the York Estate. Well, Jorjana and I relaxed on chaise lounges as we watched Franklin walk back and forth along the bluff, BB gun in hand, hunting trespassing gophers.

David worked himself into a frenzy ensuring Jorjana's comfort.

"Sit down, David," I told him. "Jorjana is fine."

David wasn't so sure. He retucked the blanket under Jorjana's feet. He stood back and looked her over from head to toe.

"I'll get some tea," he said, as much to himself as to us. And off he trotted in the direction of the kitchen.

Jorjana and I watched him go.

"He means well," Jorjana said.

"He does," I agreed.

Jorjana had been home for a week. But she was fragile at first and not up for visitors. The second her nurse called to say she wanted to see us, David and I arrived on the doorstep.

"Tell me what I have not heard. Do not spare me," Jorjana said.

I took a deep breath. Information had come in from so many sources that I had only just figured it out myself. I decided to start with Graham Tuttle—the spoke in the wheel of the story.

"Graham Tuttle's teenage son impregnated a Mexican girl back in the day, and Graham got the girl and her family deported.

215

She and the baby died during childbirth, and his son committed suicide after that. Graham managed to turn his grief over his son into rage against illegal immigrants. He's pushed for tougher legislation without success, so the next step was to find a gubernatorial candidate who would follow his agenda. He thought Ken was the perfect guy. Ken is so disorganized he comes across as an idiot. And Graham knew that Ken had made the stupid mistake of getting involved with Jesus Rodriquez and the car-theft ring."

"I was saddened to learn of Ken's poor judgment," Jorjana said.

"He is scatterbrained, and he made some really bad decisions," I said. "However..."

I told her of Ken visiting the stricken guests in the hospital and of his offer to help Fred. In spite of everything I'd learned about Ken Wheeler, I felt he was a decent man. I still thought he was a Nitwit, but a good guy underneath it all.

"His decency is what drew me to him," Jorjana said.

"Anyway, Graham figured he could control Ken, but he figured wrong. Ken didn't like the direction Graham and his cronies were steering him in. Ken tried to strike out on his own, and Graham didn't like it. He tried to rein Ken in by telling him that Jesus Rodriquez was out to get him."

"By arranging to put rhubarb in the salad and blaming this Rodriquez fellow," Jorjana said.

Jorjana seemed to be pretty up to speed on the details. I wondered why she'd asked for the update in the first place. She motioned for me to continue.

"Yeah, but before that, Graham set Rodriquez up in Stockton with the intent to get the guy thrown back in jail. Then Spencer got into trouble so Graham sent Jack Jessup in to clean up that mess. Things got hairy when Rodriquez tried to blackmail Spencer."

"Graham's scheme backfired," Jorjana said.

"You know all of this already," I accused her. "Why are you making me rehash everything?"

Jorjana blushed. "I spoke with Ken this morning. I am comparing his story to yours."

"Why?"

"While I am greatly disappointed in Ken's involvement with Jesus Rodriquez, I still believe he offers much-needed leadership. I wished to test his truthfulness before continuing my support of his campaign."

I understood her caution. She had thrown her support fully behind the guy, and he turned out to be less than perfect. Even without the catastrophe the dinner had turned into, Jorjana was wise to be wary.

"Did his story match mine?" I asked.

"Yes. Every detail. As outrageous as it all seems." Jorjana's attention turned toward the bluff. I followed her gaze.

Franklin continued his walk back and forth, BB gun in hand, eyes searching for the errant gopher or two.

As Jorjana watched Franklin, my mind wandered back to Ken Wheeler. His campaign had resumed in San Diego, with Lara by his side and Spencer's injuries repeatedly explained away as a target shooting accident that occurred while the family was in Malibu. The public was so giddy about handsome Ken Wheeler that they forgot about the who/what/where/why of the poisoned salads. And the cops sure weren't talking about their investigations. Not that anyone asked them.

The photogenic Wheeler family graced the cover of every magazine in the state. The editions flew off the shelves as the press fawned over the story of a small-town boy who grew tall, handsome, and successful.

Jorjana sighed.

"What will become of this?" she asked. "Graham is still missing?"

"He is, and his people weren't talking. But the police did follow up on Ken's suspicions, and the lab was able to trace the rhubarb to the Tuttle Estate farm. The threat of prison time loosened a few tongues. And then the police found the bodies…"

"Those poor men," Jorjana said.

"Yeah, it's tough," I said.

"And what of Mac McDonald? Rusty tells me he will not be incarcerated."

"He made a deal of some sort. I have a feeling he knows more about the drone attack than he let on. It also helped that Fred and I both said that he didn't order those guys shot. He was as shocked as we were."

"There is much blame to be spread around," Jorjana said.

"No kidding," I agreed. "Graham and Jack Jessup were a dangerous pair, but the Wheelers aren't exactly innocent bystanders. Alan told me that most of the advisors are still on board with the campaign plans. I can't say I am surprised given how well everything has been hushed up. The cops, the press, it's unbelievable. I agree with you that Ken has leadership potential but you might want to think twice about getting too close to his campaign again."

Jorjana did not respond right away. She fussed with the blanket around her legs. She fluffed her hair. She glanced over at Franklin. I could tell her feelings were torn. I also knew how loyal she was. I suspected she would continue to support Ken in one way or another.

"What did Aesop say?" Jorjana mused. "Those who are caught are not always the most guilty?"

"Seems appropriate," I said as I wondered where Graham Tuttle was hiding as Mac McDonald did a fast dance to stay out of jail.

We sat in silence while gazing at the view over Bella's Bluff. It was one of those perfect Malibu days—blue skies and full-on sunshine. The kind of day that made you count your blessings. My blessings had been counted so often in recent days that they practically lined themselves up all on their own.

"I was saddened to learn that you and Stan are no longer seeing each other," Jorjana said. "Are you certain this is the right path?"

"I'm sure," I said. "Stan's kids and his job are always going to come first. I don't want to be third place in someone's life. I want to come first."

"I understand," Jorjana said.

"Even if we did stay together, by the time the youngest one goes to college, I will be almost sixty years old!"

"Good heavens! Imagine being almost sixty years old!" Jorjana laughed.

I had the good manners to be embarrassed. Jorjana would be sixty within the month. Which gave me a great idea on how to entice our Malibu friends back to a party at the York Estate.

"Let's make big plans for your birthday," I said. "I'm thinking..."

"Darlings, I have refreshments!" David interrupted. He set a tray down on the table between Jorjana and me. The tray held four glasses of champagne.

Franklin lay down his gun and joined us.

"David, it's only ten o'clock in the morning!" Jorjana pretended to be shocked.

"It's five o'clock somewhere, darling!"

THE END

ACKNOWLEDGMENTS

I've heard other writers say that writing each book is as different from the other as each of your children differs from the other. If that's the case, *The Most Guilty* was my difficult child. I embarked on this story after the death of my mother and found myself fighting writer's block on an epic level. Without the help of the following people, I couldn't have finished the story.

La mia gratitudine e l'amore:
Claudette Sutherland, editor and teacher
Futsuki Downs, Pauline Fitzgerald, and Carl and Cindy Leroux, readers and advisors
Steve Almond, writer, teacher, and motivator
Sue Buske, eagle-eyed proofreader and friend
Martin Simonetti, husband and patron of my art

I set my stories in Malibu because I fell in love with the place over twenty-five years ago. When my son was a toddler, he and I spent endless days on the Malibu beaches digging sand castles and shooing the seagulls away from our sandwiches. That toddler is now a grown man. I once taught him the intricacies of sand castle building; he now teaches me the complexities of digital marketing. The student is now the teacher. This one is for you, son...Luv ya!

ABOUT THE AUTHOR

M. A. Simonetti is a woman of a certain age who divides her time between the beaches of SoCal and the Sonoran Desert. She is a graduate of the University of Washington Mystery Writing Series. She blogs weekly about #LifeAtaCertainAge.

The Most Guilty is her third novel.
Visit her website at www.masimonetti.com.

Made in the USA
San Bernardino, CA
16 May 2017